A TOWN FULL OF KILLERS

The territory was booming with oil and every drifter in the West was heading into Echo to grab his share.

Slade knew he would have his hands full keeping the peace—but when the phantom killer began his campaign of terror, robbery and murder, the big Ranger realized he was riding a death trail against a man who would stop at nothing!

DATE
WITH
DEATH

BRADFORD SCOTT

PYRAMID BOOKS • NEW YORK

DATE WITH DEATH

A PYRAMID BOOK

First printing March, 1969

This book is fiction. No resemblance is intended between any character herein and any person, living or dead; any such resemblance is purely coincidental.

Copyright © 1969 by Pyramid Publications, Inc.

All Rights Reserved

Printed in the United States of America

PYRAMID BOOKS are published by Pyramid Publications, Inc., 444 Madison Avenue, New York, New York 10022, U.S.A.

It was a sleepy late summer afternoon, and **ONE** Sanderson, squatting in its deep canyon, one wall of which hung over the main street, was as quiet as Sanderson ever got, almost. Even the clang and jangle and thud of the railroad yards and the hum of the big machine shop, Sanderson being a repair and change point on the east-west railroad, seemed to have acquired a drowsy note.

In Hardrock Hogan's big Branding Pen Saloon there was but a scattering of patrons at the bar, quite different from what it would be a few hours hence. The patrons dawdled over their drinks and conversed in low tones. They too appeared affected by the general somnolence.

And then, smashing the peace and quiet to smithereens, a wild-eyed man galloped a foaming horse into town. He unforked, hitched his panting mount to a rack, and dashed into the Branding Pen, nearly taking the swinging doors off their hinges.

"They did it again!" he bawled.

There were startled exclamations as everybody snapped to attention.

"What the devil are you talking about?" shouted Hardrock. "Did what again?"

"They've done struck oil again, about fifteen miles north of Tumble, that's what they've done," replied the informant. "And Westbrook Lerner, who opened up the Tumble field, says it's a big one. They're already started building a town. Going to call it Echo, after Echo Canyon."

"For the love of Pete!" bellowed a ranch owner who happened to be present. "That'll mean more trouble. More wideloopers, more dirt and smoke and smells. And more outlaws traipsin' in from all over, as if we didn't have enough as is! Why the blankety-blank blinkin' blue blazes was oil ever invented!"

"But it'll be good for business," said Hardrock, rubbing his hands together complacently. "Them oil field workers make good money, and they'll be spending a lot of it in Sanderson."

5

The ranch owner snorted digustedly and subsided to grunts and grumbles until another idea struck him.

"And I suppose Jaggers Dunn will be extending his blasted railroad from Tumble to up there, which won't help either," he growled.

"And chances are Mary Merril will be running another carting train up there, like she does for Tumble."

"Mary's all right," somebody else observed. "A good business woman, and a real fine gal too."

"Yep, she's all of that," agreed the ranch owner. "They don't come any better. A real lady, too, and purty as a little red wagon."

"Wonder if Sheriff Crane has heard about it," somebody remarked. "He'll bust a cinch."

"Old Tom's got troubles enough as is, with all the Big Bend owlhoots congregating in the section," somebody else said.

"You're darn right," growled Hardrock. "Well, to celebrate we'll all have one on the house."

"And I suppose you'll open up another rumhole up there and call it Branding Pen Three, eh? And still hang onto Branding Pen Two in Tumble?"

Hardrock grinned and didn't commit himself.

As the sunset afterglow faded, another man rode into Sanderson, a very tall, broad-shouldered man with thick, crisp black hair and pale gray eyes. He did not gallop, but the long, swinging stride of his magnificent black horse ate up more miles than did the average cayuse's gallop.

"Well, Shadow," Ranger Walt Slade, named by the *peónes* of the Rio Grande river villages *El Halcón*—The Hawk—said to the horse, "here we are in Sanderson again. And I've a notion we are going to do a mite of business here before you shake the dust of the pueblo from your hoofs. Yes, considerable bobbery in the making, as our friends the colored folks would say. First off, though, is a hefty helping of chuck for me and a full nosebag for you. Will come in mighty handy about now. So stop your fussing and sift sand."

Shadow, who was not fussing, snorted derisively, but with the prospect of oats in the offing, did quicken his pace a trifle.

First stop was a stable, where the old Mexican keeper

had a warm greeting for both man and horse and a low bow for *El Halcón*.

"And *Capitán* is again with us," he said. "Dios be praised! And the beautiful *caballo!*" He stretched out a fearless hand, and Shadow, a one-man horse who allowed nobody to put a hand on him without his master's sanction, thrust his velvety nose into the wrinkled old palm and blew softly.

"Ha! He remembers!" the keeper chortled happily.

"He never forgets an *amigo,*" Slade said. "Once your friend, always your friend."

In a trice the rig was stripped off and the big horse led into a comfortable stall and a very generous helping of oats."

"And what is *Capitán's* wish?" the keeper asked.

"A towel, a bar of soap, and a little of the water from the trough in back," Slade said.

Towel and soap were quickly forthcoming, and after a sluice in the icy waters of the trough and a clean shirt and overalls from his saddle pouches, Slade felt greatly refreshed.

"And now I'll amble over to the Reagan House and register for a room," he told the keeper. "Expect I can tie onto one."

He did, without difficulty, and in it stowed his pouches and his big Winchester rifle, a long-range special. He made sure his heavy Colt forty-fives, the plain black handles of which protruded from the holsters of the double cartridge belts circling his lean waist, were smooth in their sheaths, an instinctive gesture. A few minutes later he pushed through the swinging doors of the Branding Pen. Hardrock Hogan took one look and came ploughing across the room, hand outstretched.

Hardrock was not, at first sight, a prepossessing-looking person. He was big and burly, had an underslung jaw, a wide, almost reptilian mouth, a crooked nose, bristling red hair, and narrowed eyes of palest green. But Slade liked and respected him, for he was a square shooter in every sense of the word. A former prospector who had made a good strike and invested the proceeds in the Branding Pen Saloon, he had made a real strike, the place catching on at once and staying the most popular establishment of its kind in Sanderson. And when the oil strike to the

7

southeast blossomed forth the town of Tumble, he had opened another, calling it Branding Pen Two, which was also a moneymaker. He would have been a rich man did he not give away so much money to folks who needed it. But, as he was wont to say, he made out.

"Well, this is plumb fine!" he rumbled, shaking hands with vigor. "Mr. Slade! Back with us a while, eh? You know, when I heard about the new oil strike a little while ago, I straightway had a notion you'd be showing up in the section soon. Guess you heard about it 'fore us fellers did."

Slade did, but didn't say so; he merely smiled. Hardrock bumbled on.

"Sheriff Crane will be tickled pink. He was in a mighty bad temper when he left, after hearing about the strike. Reckon he'll feel a mite better now. But I guess you're hungry. Here's your favorite table, by the dance floor. Will hold it for you while you're in the section. I'm for the kitchen. Just wait till the boys learn who they're serving tonight." He hustled off. A moment later the kitchen door opened a crack and the cook and his helpers, all Mexican, bowed to *El Halcón* and waved greetings, which Slade answered.

Now the Branding Pen was filling up fast, the oil strike the prevailing topic of discussion, some lauding, some deploring, a decided difference of opinion, and sometimes heated. Slade listened with interest.

After consuming a bountiful and tasty meal and a quiet after-dinner smoke, Slade visited the kitchen to thank the cook and his boys in flawless Spanish for the really excellent repast, leaving them wreathed with smiles. Then, waving so long to Hardrock, he made his way to the sheriff's office. The door was closed, but a light burned inside. He pushed open the door and entered.

Rugged old Sheriff Tom Crane looked up from his desk, his eyes widening, and leaped to his feet with a joyous bellow.

"Well, I'll be hanged! Might have known it, you and trouble always come together. How are you, Walt? I was wishing you were here when I heard about that blankety-blank oil strike. Was getting ready to write McNelty a letter. How come you show up so handy?"

"Captain Jim and Jaggers Dunn were having a confab

and invited me to sit in," Slade replied. (The Captain Jim in question was Captain Jim McNelty, the famed Commander of the Border Battalion of the Texas Rangers. Jaggers Dunn, the equally famed James G. Dunn, was General Manager of the great C. & P. Railroad System.)

"Wait till I get you some coffee from the back room and then you can turn your wolf loose on me," said the sheriff.

The coffee was soon forthcoming and Slade continued.

"Westbrook Lerner wrote Mr. Dunn, informing him what he had in mind. Dunn wired him to go ahead and promised cooperation. They figured it might be a good notion for me to stick around the section for a while, in case there might be need of a little Texas Ranger authority, or maybe *El Halcón* authority, and here I am. Now you can give me the lowdown on things in general."

"First," growled Crane, "I figure you're the one really to blame for that oil strike. I recall you telling Lerner that there was very likely another seepage pool north of Tumble. That was enough to set him off."

"Chances are he'd have discovered it sooner or later," Slade replied. "He's a top flight oilman."

"Maybe," the sheriff conceded, but not appearing overly impressed. "He—Hell and Blazes!"

The exclamation was fairly shot from him as the windows clang-jangled, the shingles ground together, and the whole building rocked to the shattering roar of an explosion not far off.

For a moment both Slade and the sheriff sat stunned at the unexpected suddenness of it. Then **TWO** Slade surged to his feet.

"Was over by the canyon wall," he said as they rushed out the door.

"A big fire over there, too," chattered the sheriff. "Look at it blaze!"

In every direction cursing, shouting men were running toward the scene of the conflagration. The sheriff started to join them, but Slade stopped him.

"Hold it!" he said. "Something funny about this. Nothing over there to blow up or burn. Listen! Hear that? A shot, sort of muffled like it was inside, and right around the corner. Come on!"

"Nothing on that block 'cept Vanstaveren's big general store," said Crane as they raced to the corner and whisked around it. "Look, a light in his office. Everything else dark."

"Steady," Slade cautioned. "The door is a trifle open. Ease ahead and perhaps we can see what's going on. I think I know. Get ready for business." He led the way to the two steps that led to the door, glided up them, slammed the door wide open, and saw what he expected to see.

On the floor lay a grayhaired man, his face crimsoned by blood that flowed from a head wound. Another grizzled man knelt beside a big iron safe, twirling the combination knob. Over him loomed a man with hatbrim pulled low, neckerchief looped high, and a gun in his hand. Not far from a door that led into the main store room stood three more masked men, hands close to their holsters. They whirled at the sound of the opening door and went for their guns.

But Slade drew and shot with both hands before they could clear leather, his big Colts booming like thunder.

One of the robbers fell. The sheriff's gun cracked and another went down. The third man by the door, tall, bulky, dashed through the door and into the main store room. A wild shot smashed the single bracket lamp light. In the second before darkness swooped down, Slade and the robber by the safe squeezed trigger at almost the same instant. *El Halcón* reeled slightly as a slug barely touched his left cheekbone, but the outlaw plunged forward onto his face.

Steps were beating through the main room. A door banged open. Slade started to pursue the fleeing outlaw, but desisted. There was no guarantee that the three down were dead. Only wounded, they would still be capable of some fanging.

"Hold it!" he told the sheriff, who was still blazing away in the general direction of the door.

Silence followed, save a beat of fast hoofs outside, fading into the distance.

"Slaven, you all right?" the sheriff called.

"Okay," came the reply from the floor beside the safe. "All right to stand up?"

"Just a minute," Slade said. He flipped a match alight with his thumbnail and extinguished it in almost the same instant. The tiny flicker showed three motionless forms on the floor, from which there was nothing more to fear. The grizzled man by the safe was also stretched out on the floor.

"Everything under control," Slade decided. "Get a light going, please." There was a scuffling about and a glow filled the room.

Slade spared the dead outlaws but a single glance and then knelt beside the man with the head wound, exploring the vicinity of the gash with sensitive fingers.

"No indications of fracture, so far as I can ascertain," he said. "Should be coming out of it soon."

"That's Vanstaveren on the floor," put in the sheriff. "The other old coot is Slaven, his partner. What the devil happened, Slaven?"

"Happened so fast I can hardly tell you," the grizzled man answered. "We were just getting ready to tally the week's take when those devils barged in through the front door that was supposed to be locked but I reckon wasn't. Van made a grab for his gun in the drawer, and the big one in front shot him. He ordered me to open the safe. I didn't argufy with him and was beginning to twirl the knob when you fellers showed up at just the right time.

11

We're sure beholden to you. Plenty of *dinero* in the safe, and I got a sorta feeling those sidewinders ain't the sort that leave witnesses alive."

Slade thought he was very likely right. "Might be a good notion to bank your take every day instead of letting it pile up and be a temptation to gentlemen with share-the-wealth notions," he commented.

"Guess you're right there," Slaven admitted. "Say, you're Mr. Slade, Tom's special deputy, ain't you? Remember you being pointed out to me when you were here a while back. Mighty glad to see you."

"You'll always see him where there's trouble," growled the sheriff. "It follows him around like flies after a sugar barrel."

"Uh-huh, and he takes care of it; no doubt in my mind as to that," declared Slaven.

Now shouts were sounding outside, and the pad of running feet. The barrage of gunfire had been heard and had attracted everybody who didn't happen to be congregated at the canyon wall. Another moment and cautious heads poked in the door.

"Come on in and take a look," the sheriff called.

"And somebody fetch the doctor," Slade added. "Mr. Vanstaveren is hurt." A couple of men dashed off to care for the chore. The others crowded in, exclaiming, questioning.

"What was burning over by the canyon wall?" Slade asked.

"Just a big pile of dry brush," somebody replied. "Wasn't anything blowed down, so far as we could see."

Slade nodded. "A smart bunch," he told the sheriff. "Set off a stick or two of dynamite and fired the brush to attract everybody from the vicinity of the store, so they could operate without interruption. Looks like we might be up against something, Tom."

"Anyhow, only one got away," said Crane. Slade had his own opinion anent that, but didn't remark.

"And it came very nearly being successful," he said.

"Would have been if you hadn't caught on so fast," grunted Crane. "All right, some of you work dodgers, pack those carcasses to my office and lay 'em on the floor. We'll be along shortly. Deputy Charley Blount should be there. He'll let you in."

12

There were plenty of volunteers for the chore and very soon the grim cortege got under way, the chattering crowd stringing along behind. They reached the office and Deputy Blount, who was on duty there, opened up and the room was soon packed.

"All right, anybody see 'em before?" Crane asked.

There was no worthwhile response until a Tumble bartender who was visiting kinfolks in Sanderson spoke up.

"I saw 'em before, Sheriff," he said. "About three weeks back they came into my place, and two more of the same sort. I noticed 'em particular 'cause I thought they were all ornery looking scuts, and because they kept talking real low with their heads drawed together and peerin' this way and that like they were checkin' the place. I whispered to the boss and he sat in the back room with a sawed-off shotgun ready for business. But they didn't try to pull anything, just had a few drinks and left."

"Did you see them again?" Slade asked.

"Nope, and I didn't want to," the drink juggler replied. "They gave me a sorta funny feeling."

"Did you notice anything unusual about the other two?"

The barkeep shook his head. "Nothing except one of them was taller and bigger than the others."

"And the one who got away tonight was taller and bigger than those three on the floor," the sheriff interpolated.

"Thank you," Slade said to the bartender. "What you told us may prove helpful."

"And I reckon that's all," said Crane. "Okay, outside everybody; we got work to do."

With the door locked and the window blind drawn, they examined the bodies. Their pockets divulged nothing of interest save a quite large sum of money. Their hands indicated all three had at one time or another been cowhands, but not recently. Typical Big Bend outlaws, was Slade's summing up. More intelligent than the average, utterly ruthless.

"Hellions have been doing all right by themselves," the sheriff remarked as he stowed the money in his safe. "We'll take that up later. Somebody at the door. See who it is, Charley."

Deputy Blount opened the door to admit Doc Cooper. The old frontier practitioner shook hands with Slade.

"Vanstaveren is all right except for a sore head, just

13

creased," he announced. "No indications of fracture or concussion, eh Walt?"

"None I could ascertain," Slade agreed.

"Then there isn't any," said Doc. "Your hands are never wrong. Blazes! What a surgeon was lost when you decided to be—something else."

"Uh-huh, and plenty of folks with the knowhow will tell you grand opera lost a plumb bright star when instead of singing on a stage he started using that voice of his to beller 'Hands up!' to owlhoots."

"The singingest man in the whole Southwest, with the fastest gunhand," chuckled Doc.

"And gents like Jaggers Dunn, oil millionaire Jim Hogg, who used to be a Texas Governor, and 'Bet a Million' Gates of Wall Street will tell you he's the best engineer that ever rode across Texas."

"Hold it!" Slade said laughingly. "You're giving me the undeserved reputation that I'll go loco trying to live up to."

However, the sheriff was not far off from the truth. Shortly before the death of his father, which happened after financial reverses resulted in the loss of the elder Slade's ranch, young Walt had graduated with high honors from a noted college of engineering. He had expected to take a post-graduate course in certain subjects to round out his education and better fit him for the profession he hoped to make his life's work. That being impossible at the moment, he was sort of at loose ends and couldn't decide which way to turn. So when Captain Jim McNelty, with whom Slade had worked some during summer vacations, suggested he sign up with the Rangers for a while and pursue his studies in spare time, Slade decided the notion was a good one.

So Walt Slade became a Texas Ranger. Long since, he had gotten more from private study than he could have hoped for from the post-grad and was eminently fitted for the profession of engineering.

But meanwhile Ranger work had gotten a strong hold on him, providing as it did so many opportunities to right wrongs, help the deserving, bring malefactors to justice, and make the land he loved a better land for good people. He was loath to sever connections with the illustrious body of law-enforcement officers. He was

14

young, plenty of time to be an engineer. He'd stick with the Rangers for a while longer.

Doc Cooper, who was also coroner, glanced at the clock. "I'll hold an inquest on those carcasses tomorrow evening," he promised. "Too late to do anything tonight. Be seeing you, gents."

"And I," said Slade, "am going to bed. We'll get together for a powwow tomorrow, Tom."

Without misadventure he reached his hotel room, tumbled into bed, and was almost immediately asleep.

The morning was well along when Slade awoke, greatly rested, fit for anything, and hungry. To care for which lack he made his way to the Branding Pen, where he found Sheriff Crane awaiting him, fortified by a full glass.

"Figured you'd be dropping in about now," the sheriff said. "Let us eat!"

Which they proceeded to do, bountifully. The saloon was buzzing over the frustrated robbery of the night before, and admiring glances were bent on Slade. But Hardrock allowed nobody to approach them, so they were able to enjoy a leisurely breakfast without interruption.

"And now," Slade said as he sipped a final cup of steaming coffee, "suppose you give me the lowdown on what's been going on that's got you worked up."

"Plenty," growled Crane. "Nothing plumb unusual like what was pulled last night, what with setting off dynamite and firing a brush heap to get everybody away from the store. Just routine robberies, burglings, shootings, cow stealing, but plenty bad. A really bad one at Langtry, to the east of here. Rumhole held up right after closing time, bartender shot dead. I'm sure for certain it was the same bunch that's been operating hereabouts. Over on the railroad street a rumhole was held up in the same way. Nobody killed, thank Pete. Owner clubbed unconscious, safe cleaned. Another one on Main Street. Floor man shot through the shoulder. Two shops on Main Street burgled, slick work. All the spreads claim to be losing cows. Of course they've always lost some now and then, but nothing like what they say they have in the past month."

"Sounds like a repeat of conditions the last time I was here," Slade commented. "Any notion as to their identity?"

Crane shook his head. "That's the worst part of it. 'Pears

15

nobody has got a really good look at the devils, except for these three on the floor, and that after they were dead. Maybe there's two or three bunches working the section."

"I rather doubt it," Slade said. "The depredations appear to follow a definite pattern."

"Guess that's right," Crane conceded. "Well, you cleaned up the hellions the last time you were here, and I figure this will be another repeat, as you call it."

"Hope you're right," Slade replied. "How are conditions down at Tumble?"

"Just about as bad as here," Crane growled. "Rumhole or two robbed, and several shops. Couple of oil workers killed, for what they had in their pockets, I reckon. Yes, just as bad or worse than used to be there, with the new oil strike coming along to complicate matters. Do you figure the one who made it in the clear last night was all left of the bunch?"

"Definitely no," Slade answered. "I fear you'll learn we are up against a rather large outfit with, per usual, a shrewd and capable individual heading it."

"Think the one that got away is the head snake?"

"It is possible, even probable. The manner in which he made his escape denoted quick thinking and an instant grasp of opportunity. And the complicated manner in which the try was made was the sort of thing one might expect the brains of the bunch to handle in person."

"Well, the sidewinder is due to learn what it means to be up against real brains, the brains of *El Halcón*," Crane grunted, downing his drink and hammering for a refill.

"Your confidence is inspiring," Slade smiled. "I'm going back to the kitchen and thank the boys for taking care of us so well."

As he sauntered across the room, the sheriff thought what a fine looking young man he was, and how he stood out in the crowd.

Walt Slade was very tall, more than six feet, **THREE**
and the breadth of his shoulders and the depth
of his chest were in keeping with his splendid height.

His face was as striking as his form. A rather wide
mouth, grin-quirked at the corners, relieved somewhat the
tinge of fierceness evinced by the prominent hawk nose
above and the powerful jaw and chin beneath.

The sternly handsome countenance was dominated by
long, black-lashed eyes of very pale gray. Cold, reckless
eyes that nevertheless always seemed to have gay little
devils of laughter dancing in their clear depths. Devils
that could, did occasion warrant, leap to the front and
become anything but laughter. Then those eyes became
"The Terrible Eyes of *El Halcón*" before whose bleak
glare gentlemen with the reputation of being plenty
salty were known to back down in a hurry.

Slade wore the plain, efficient garb of the rangeland
—Levis, the bibless overalls favored by cowhands, soft
blue shirt with vivid neckerchief looped at the throat,
well-scuffed half-boots of softly tanned leather, and the
broad-brimmed J.B.—the rainshed of the plains—and wore
it as great Coronado must have worn armor.

Around his sinewy waist were double cartridge belts,
from the carefully worked and oiled cut-out holsters
of which protruded the plain black butts of heavy guns,
and from these big Colts his slender, muscular hands
seemed never far away.

Slade chatted with the kitchen help for some time and,
incidentally, enlisted their help in identifying and running
down the mysterious outlaw bunch. Help that past experience taught him was not to be discounted. After which
he returned to the sheriff.

"And now what?" Crane asked.

"Now I think I'll ride up to the new oil field for a
look-see," Slade replied.

Crane looked interested. "Mind if I ride with you?"

"Be glad to have you," *El Halcón* said.

17

_"Can't help but think somebody might have a notion to try and even up for last night," Crane explained. "If so, two is better'n one." The truth of which Slade was willing to admit. And the rugged old peace officer was good company did the going get rough. Without delay they saddled up and set out.

"I predict you'll be surprised at the progress made," Slade remarked. "Lerner felt sure that when Dunn got back from a European trip he would agree to cooperate. So, unbeknown to folks at Tumble he began to make preparations some time ago. He was able to make some profitable deals at Fort Stockton and had wagons loaded with machinery and materials ready to roll as soon as he got the go ahead from Dunn. Workers signed up, too, and they've been working like beavers for some days now. Only yesterday did Tumble folks learn for sure what was really going on."

"Sounds like him and Dunn," snorted the sheriff. "You, too, of course, the real promoter of the deal." Slade laughed and did not argue the point.

Soon they were riding across big ranches where fat beefs grazed. Several times they saw, in the distance, cowhands going about their chores.

"Wonder how the ranchers are going to take to the railroad crossing their land and the new field raising heck?" the sheriff observed.

"Something for us to keep in mind," Slade answered. "Remember, there was trouble between the ranchers and the oilmen right after the Tumble field was opened."

"Which you squelched," Crane said. "I figure as was in the past, so it will be in the future."

"Hope you're right," Slade smiled. A little later he pointed to a dark smudge fouling the clean blue of the Texas sky.

"And there's your new oil field, right under that smoke," he said.

The field lay in a great basin surrounded by low hills, those to the south being considerably lower than those buttressing the other three sides of the bowl.

Except to the north where there was but a thin straggle, the crests and slopes were heavily brush-grown.

"There will have to be a cut made through those bumps on the ground to accommodate the railroad right-of-way, but it shouldn't be much of a chore," Slade said. "There's a very old trail crossing them and continuing across the northern range. We follow that. I've a notion it was beaten out by the feet of Indians, or possibly by the folk who came before the red man. Hard to tell for sure."

"Yep, I can see it," replied the sheriff. "Not much more than a snake track, but makes the going easier."

They sent the horses toiling up the steep slope, crossed the wooded crest to the far sag, and the field, a scene of bustling activity, lay before them.

Already three tall derricks were erected, the walking beams doing their ponderous dance as they churned the heavy drills into the stubborn earth. Hoisting engines puffed and snorted, compressors hummed, smoke boiled from the furnaces. And everywhere saws and hammers flashed, with buildings going up under their onslaught.

"Big one over this way nearly finished," Crane remarked. "Betcha it's already housing a rumhole."

"Quite likely," Slade conceded. "Well, an old saying has it that the West was won on gunpowder and whiskey."

"And don't forget the gals," the sheriff chuckled. "They did their part, and still are." Which Slade did not argue.

After giving the horses a breathing spell they descended to the level ground. The workers regarded them curiously but did not speak.

However, they had evidently been spotted on the crest of the rise, for a man came hurrying to greet them. A vigorous little man with a leathery, poreless skin and quick bright eyes.

"Well, well, well!" exclaimed Westbrook Lerner. "Mr. Slade and the sheriff! Had a notion you'd show up soon. How's everything, Mr. Slade? Trouble still following you around, as the sheriff says?"

"I'll say it is!" snorted Crane. "He wasn't in town long enough to shake the dust off 'fore there was a darned smart robbery try and three blasted wind spiders got their comeuppance! Trouble! It's his middle name!"

"Sounds like old times," Lerner chuckled. "And the way the ranchers are growling, I wouldn't be surprised if he'll be able to do a little business here before all is said and done."

"Won't surprise me one bit," grumbled the sheriff. "I crave a snort."

"Come right along," said Lerner. "To the Diehard, as the owner calls it. Bar already in place, and stocked."

"What did I tell you?" grunted Crane as the oilman led the way to the almost completed large building they had noted from the crest. "Didn't I tell you the first one finished would be taken over by a rumhole?"

Lerner chuckled again. "Usually that way," he conceded. "Feller named Rader, Vince Rader, owns it. Must be pretty well heeled, paid to have his equipment brought in by wagon. 'Pears to be all right."

They entered the building and found themselves in a big room that was already sheathed and furnished. The long bar was shining, the back bar pyramided with bottles. There was a dance floor, a lunch counter, chairs and tables, and a couple of roulette wheels. Everything appeared to be spotlessly clean. Without doubt Vince Rader was a good saloon man.

"Going to partition off sleeping rooms upstairs when they get the second floor finished," Lerner observed. "That's Rader at the far end of the bar, talking to the bartender. Slade regarded the Diehard owner with interest.

Vince Rader was a big man, tall and broad, and gave the impression of being solidly built. His features were hewn, but more than passably good looking in a rugged way. His hair was dark, and so were his eyes. Keen, alert eyes, Slade thought.

Rader came forward to greet them. "Gents," Lerner said, "this is Vince Rader who owns these diggin's. Rader, I want you to know Sheriff Tom Crane and Mr. Walt Slade, his special deputy. We're going to take a chance on a little of your snake juice."

"Fine!" replied Rader, his voice deep and nicely modulated. "And with every third glass you get a free snake. Everything on the house, of course. Got to keep on the right side of the law." He shook hands with a good grip, and added, "If you feel the need of a surrounding, we've got the kitchen functioning after a fashion and will try to accommodate. Nothing elaborate as I expect to have later, but enough to make out, I venture to say."

He motioned to a smiling waiter who conducted them to a table and took their orders.

"See you later," Rader said, and returned to the far end of the bar.

"Has nice people working for him, always pleasant," Lerner remarked. "I've a notion he is a good man to work for."

The "snake juice" was soon forthcoming, and Crane pronounced it prime.

"Gent's a good judge of whiskey, too, which is to his credit," was his verdict. "Too many rumhole owners ain't. Waiter! Let's have another one. How about you fellers?"

Lerner risked another snort. Slade settled for coffee, which the cook delivered in person, with a low bow to *El Halcón*.

Slade thanked him in Spanish, and he returned to his kitchen beaming.

The Diehard was filling up. With oil workers and builders, Slade decided. A gay, chattery crowd, mostly young, although there were some gray heads scattered about. The sheriff glanced around at the well-laid-out place and chuckled.

"Sorta different from what was usual in the old days when a boom town got going. Then a shed over a long plank laid on a coupla barrels, with packing cases for a back bar was the order."

Lerner laughed. "Well, we have got one of something on that nature," he said. "The Wallop, up to the north end of town, though they do have walls and a roof up. Like to drop in there before we go to my place?"

"Not a bad idea," Slade agreed.

As they were finishing their drink, Rader sauntered over and wanted to buy another.

"Guess we've had all we can handle for the time being," the sheriff declined. His companions nodded agreement.

"Come back soon," Rader requested. They promised to do so.

Passing along streets that Lerner had insisted be laid out in orderly squares, their horses pacing after them, they finally approached another rather large structure, over which builders were swarming.

"Fellow named Frederick Norton owns the place," Lerner said. "He came to me and asked permission to go into business. Didn't see any reason why he shouldn't, so

21

I donated the land and told him to go ahead." Slade knew that Lerner, with his usual generosity, had thrown the field wide open to all comers, first come first served.

The room they entered was nearly as large as that of the Diehard, but quite different in furnishings. The long bar, while brightly polished, was plainly of homemade construction, oaken planks. The back bar of the same, as yet devoid of a mirror, although there were strippings to accommodate one. There was the beginning of a lunch counter. Three doors led from the main room. One at the far end of the bar doubtless led to a back room that served as an office and for the storing of stock. Another, to the kitchen under construction. A third, to a dressing room to accommodate the dance-floor girls. Or so Slade reasoned. A few remarks by Lerner a little later confirmed his deductions.

"There comes Norton out of the back room," Lerner said as a waiter led them to one of the few tables already on the floor and took their orders with a smile and a bow.

The dance floor was spaced out, and on a little raised platform over to one side a Mexican orchestra was tuning up.

"Jigger has the right notion," the sheriff remarked. "Whiskey and gals first things and you're all set to go."

Slade was rather surprised to note quite a few cowhands at the bar.

"They seem to have sorta took to the place," Lerner replied when he commented on the fact. "Don't have to ride all the way to Tumble or Sanderson for a drink and a dance with a girl. Keep to themselves and behave, at least so far. It's the owners who do the grumbling; the hands don't give the field or the coming railroad much thought. Was that way, to an extent, at Tumble before you made peace between the factions.

"Maybe the name of the place attracts the rannies," he added. "Wallop is a brand, is it not?"

"That's right," Slade answered. "A burn with a rather stirring history. You might have something there."

"Norton's coming over to say hello," Lerner said. Slade regarded the Wallop owner with interest.

Frederick Norton was rather taller than average, with shoulders to more than match his height. He had a straight-featured face, his nose prominent, as was his chin. His

22

mouth gave an impression of firmness. His eyes, Slade noted as he drew near, were light blue and set deep in his head. His stride was lithe, almost graceful. His voice, when he acknowledged Lerner's introduction of his companions, was rather high-pitched, but not unmusical.

"Wanted the sheriff and Mr. Slade, his special deputy, to have a look at your place," Lerner said. "You're coming along, all right."

"Yes, I hope to have my kitchen ready for business in a few more days," Norton replied. "Keeps me scratching, though. Costs money to fit up a place," he added with a wry smile. "Oh, I'm not complaining. I'm already doing quite well, and expect to do even better before long."

The waiter arrived with their drinks. Norton jerked his thumb toward the ceiling, which meant, of course, "on the house."

The waiter's smile broadened as he pocketed the generous tip Slade pressed into his hand.

"Have a couple more," Norton invited. But the sheriff, interpreting Slade's quick glance, declined.

"Much obliged, but I'm scairt we haven't time for more than one," he said. "Want to take a look at Lerner's diggin's 'fore we ride. We'll be seeing you again."

"Make it soon, please," Norton requested.

"Chances are we will," Crane predicted. "Got a notion we'll be in this pueblo quite often."

Lerner, an unpretentious man despite his wealth, had a modest dwelling, one of the first erected, consisting of a sleeping room with bunks for three, a cubbyhole office, and a small kitchen. There was an unfinished second floor.

"It'll be a dark and lonely ride," he protested when Slade announced their intention to head for Sanderson as soon as the horses emptied their nosebags.

"Not too bad," the Ranger replied. "We'll make out, isn't so very late and will be nice cool riding." Half an hour later found them on their way. The night was dark, the sky being slightly overcast. But a moon just rising in the east was already silvering the crest of the rise. They were not far from the base of the slope when Slade abruptly turned Shadow's nose east.

"What's the notion?" Crane asked as he swerved **FOUR**
his own mount.

"Tom," Slade replied, "call it a hunch or what you
will, but somehow I don't cotton to the idea of riding up
that moonlit trail with thick growth on either side. This
afternoon I noticed, over east a short distance, a spot
where the chaparral on the slope is quite thin. I'm pretty
sure the horses can make it to the crest there. On the
crest we'll use them as long as appears safe to do so,
then leave them in the brush and ease ahead on foot until
we see what's what. May sound silly, but I can't help
but feel it's the right thing to do."

"It sure is, if you feel that way," Crane agreed without hesitation. "I've got plenty of faith in your hunches."

They forged east for a few score paces. Then Slade
resumed the course to the base of the slope, the sheriff
beside him.

The horses had no difficulty negotiating the sag where
the brush was thin and very quickly reached the crest,
where Slade turned west, easing them along slowly and
almost in silence. A little farther and he drew rein.

"Leave the cayuses here," he breathed and dismounted,
dropping the split reins to the ground, which would keep
Shadow right where he was until called for. The sheriff
hitched his critter to a convenient branch. Then together
they edged along the lip of the crest toward the trail.

They had almost reached it when Slade whispered,
"Hear it? They're there, all right."

The sheriff did hear it, the faint jingle of a bridle iron
as a horse petulantly tossed its head.

The sheriff did hear it, the faint jingle of a bridle iron
as a horse petulantly tossed its head.

"The snake-blooded skunks!" he breathed. "We'd oughta
blow them down soon as we spot them."

"We're law-enforcement officers and must give them the
chance they don't deserve to surrender," Slade said. "They
won't, so shoot fast and straight. Come ahead now."

Step by slow step they crept to the edge of the growth.
Now the moon was well up in the sky, and by its light

they saw three men standing in the trail, looking over the lip of the sag. One spoke, in a querulous voice.

"Where the devil is the hellion? He'd oughta showed before now. Where is he?"

"Gents," Slade called, "he's right here. Up! You are under arrest!"

A chorus of startled exclamations! The outlaws whirled toward the sound of Slade's voice, grabbing for their holsters. But *El Halcón* drew and shot with both hands before they cleared leather. The sheriff's gun boomed echo.

Two of the drygulchers fell. The other jerked his iron and fired a wild shot before he too went down, to lie motionless. Slade peered through the powder fog at the three still forms in the dust of the trail.

"Hold it," he told Crane. "Everything under control."

"Uh-huh, and three more blasted wind spiders learned that trying to drygulch *El Halcón* is a losing game," the sheriff replied.

"It was clumsily handled," Slade said. "Seems incredible that they would believe we would come riding up the trail in the moonlight."

"Uh-huh, plumb incredible," the sheriff responded dryly. "But if it wasn't for your hunches—rather, you figuring in advance what might happen—it would have worked. I'll admit I would have done just that, as so would most anybody else. Guess they heard the shooting in the field; folks heading this way."

Men were indeed approaching the base of the sag, cautiously, shouting and swearing. Slade sent his voice rolling down to them.

"Fetch lanterns, and Mr. Lerner."

Soon the lighted lanterns were bobbing up the trail. Before they reached the crest, Slade, by the aid of a couple of matches, had given the drygulchers' hands a quick examination. He nodded with satisfaction.

Very quickly there was a crowd of oil workers clustered around the bodies, exclaiming, questioning. Slade stilled the tumult by asking a question of his own.

"Any of you fellows ever followed a cow's tail?" A couple said they had, to the accompaniment of mutters against the blankety-blank ranchers.

"Take a look at those devils' hands and tell me what you see," Slade requested.

The pair came forward and did so.

"Two of them used to be punchers but haven't worked at it for a long time; branding iron and rope marks show that," one said. "The other one never was, though there are tool marks on his hands. I'd say he maybe worked around an oil field or a railroad."

"And," Slade said, "wouldn't that absolve the ranchers of having anything to do with this drygulching try?"

"Guess that's so," the former cowboy said. There were nods of agreement.

"But Mr. Slade, if it isn't the ranchers making trouble, who is it?" the second puncher asked.

"Frankly, I don't know," Slade replied. "But I intend to find out."

"Guess he will," said a voice. More nods.

Lerner arrived, took in the situation at a glance.

"Well, this is like old times," he said. "Did those hellions try to gun you?"

"Yes, but they didn't quite make a go of it," Slade replied.

"But if he hadn't figured everything in advance they would have succeeded," said the sheriff. Admiring glances were bent on Slade.

"And that *is* like old times," chuckled Lerner, to the accompaniment of a general laugh.

"We'll pack 'em to Sanderson in a mule cart, Sheriff," Lerner promised.

"And see if you can locate their horses and put them in Mr. Lerner's stable," Slade told the workers.

Crane went through the drygulchers' pockets and unearthed a surprisingly large amount of money.

"I told you the hellions have been doing well by themselves," he remarked to Slade as he stowed it away. "Well, I see they've found the horses and are leading them down the sag. Guess that about takes care of everything here, does it not?"

"Yes," Slade agreed. "We might as well make another try for Sanderson."

"Sure you'll be safe the rest of the way?" worried Lerner.

"I don't think we need fear an encore tonight," Slade reassured him. "You take care of yourself. We'll be seeing you."

"Okay," Lerner replied. "I expect to be in Sanderson day after tomorrow. Want to have a talk with Miss Merril and persuade her to shift her cart line run to Echo. The railroad will take care of Tumble, for the time being, at least."

"She'll cooperate," Slade said.

"If you say so, I'm sure she will," Lerner smiled. "Once again, be seeing you."

He trudged down the sag, the workers streaming after him. Slade and the sheriff resumed their interrupted ride to Sanderson through a night of moonlight and a sprinkling of stars.

It lacked an hour of dawn when they reached the railroad town, and after caring for their horses they went to bed.

Well past mid-afternoon, Slade awoke rested and in a fairly complacent frame of mind. Things weren't going so bad. A robbery attempt thwarted and half a dozen owlhoots given their comeuppance. No, not so bad, so far. But the identity of the outlaws, especially the head of the bunch that Slade was confident existed, was still a mystery. The worst part being that he had not a single suspect so far. Oh well, that had been the case before, and sooner or later it had always resolved in a satisfactory manner, so why worry!

He arose, bathed, shaved, and cleaned up a bit. Gradually it dawned on him that he was hungry. Which was not remarkable, seeing as coffee and a couple of snorts was all he'd had since the previous morning. He headed for the Branding Pen and breakfast.

When he entered the saloon, Sheriff Crane was at their favorite table waiting for him.

Keeping the sheriff company, her back to the swinging doors, was a girl. She was a rather small girl, but her proportions certainly were all that could be desired, attested to by the low-cut bodice and short, spangled skirt much the same as the dance-floor girls wore.

Winking at the sheriff, Slade glided across the room with his swift, noiseless step. She gave a startled squeal as he lifted her from the floor, chair and all.

Chuckling, he let the chair fall to the floor and cradled her in his arms. She still wasn't able to get a look at his

27

face, but Miss Mary Merril was not easily thrown off balance, figuratively speaking.

"Oh, I know it's you, darling!" she said. "Nobody else would pull such a loco stunt. Besides, I saw your name on the hotel register. That's why I donned my dancing outfit, for your special benefit. Which means too, of course, that you'll have to dance with me tonight. Uncle Tom has been regaling me with an account of your latest escapades. Same old story, let you out of my sight and you're in trouble. How are you, dear?"

"Fine as froghair. And you?"

"Oh, I'm all right, only busy as a dog burying bones, as Uncle Tom would phrase it. Mr. Lerner is going to want me to shift the cart train from Tumble to Echo—they'll soon be in need of casings and other materials as they put down more wells. Of course it means a change of route, which will slow us up a little at the start. But we'll make out. Personally, the notion appeals; there is an allure to opening up a new field. Perhaps I'm just a wildcatter at heart."

"You always were in the nature of a chuck-line-riding cowhand," Slade said smilingly. "A wonder you didn't end up one."

"With a new bunkhouse every night! Wonderful!"

"And that will be enough of that out of you," Slade asserted.

"I'm hungry," Mary complained. "Put me down, darling, and let's eat."

"Come to think of it, so am I," replied Slade, dropping her into her chair.

"Second the motion," said the sheriff. "Waiter!"

"I had a feeling you would be here today," Mary said to Slade. "That's why I rode ahead of the carts. They should roll in any minute now. We won't load until tomorrow, or perhaps the next day. All depends on my talk with Mr. Lerner, although I'm pretty sure he'll want me to head for Echo instead of Tumble. We'll see. Anyhow we should have a couple of days together."

"Nights can be interesting too," commented the sheriff. Mary made a face at him.

Hardrock Hogan joined them while they were waiting for their breakfast orders to be filled.

"This is plumb fine," he said. "Just like old times. Sure wish we could keep it this way."

"Oh, you'd get tired of us after a while," Mary predicted.

"Never!" declared Hardrock. "And if I could hire you to dance and Mr. Slade to sing, I'd retire rich in six months. Whoops! Here come the carts. Now business is really going to pick up." He hustled to the back room to check stock.

They had just finished eating when Clay Saxon, the head carter, entered.

"Everything okay, Miss Mary," he reported. "Carts lined for loading, and I'm heading to the bank with a couple of the boys riding herd on me. Be seeing you, everybody."

"He don't take any chances since the time Walt kept him from losing the poke and, mighty likely, his life too, and told him off for fair," the sheriff remarked.

"A good man and dependable, but he was prone to be a mite careless," Slade observed.

"He ain't no more," Crane said cheerfully. "Let us drink!"

The carters roared in, the only word to adequately describe their entrance, and business did pick up, decidedly.

"And betcha the music makers and the gals will come on early," predicted the sheriff. He was right.

"And now that I'm no longer famished, I'm going to my room and lie down for a couple of hours; I've been up since before daybreak," Mary said. "Try and keep out of trouble till I get back, both of you."

She kissed Slade lightly, grimaced at the sheriff and trotted out.

"They don't come any better," declared Crane. "Yep, a gal to ride the river with."

Slade nodded sober agreement to the highest compliment the rangeland can pay.

"Why, look who just came in!" Crane uttered in a surprised voice.

Slade had already noted the big solidly built **FIVE**
man with rough-hewn features who had pushed
through the swinging doors. It was Vince Rader, owner of
the Diehard saloon in Echo. He glanced around, saw Slade
and the sheriff, and waved a cordial greeting, which they
acknowledged.

However, he did not approach their table but made
his way to the far end of the bar, where he shook hands
with Hardrock, who did not appear particularly surprised
at his advent.

"Would seem they are acquainted," Slade remarked.

"Uh-huh, looks that way," Crane agreed.

Hardrock and Rader conversed for quite some time,
then the Diehard owner took his leave, pausing for a
word with Slade and the sheriff.

"Going over and register for a room and get freshened
up a bit," he said. "A rather hard ride through the heat.
Be seeing you later."

Hardrock ambled across and joined Slade and the
sheriff.

"So you know Rader, eh?" Crane remarked.

"Knew him quite well some years back when we were
both prospectors," Hardrock replied. "Then he sorta
dropped out of sight and I lost track of him. Heard in
a roundabout way that he had made a good strike and
was well heeled with dinero. Didn't hear anything more
about him. Then just a month back he dropped in on me.
Said he'd heard about the Branding Pen. Said he'd like
to open up a place in this section. He had worked for a
saloonkeeper before he took to prospecting, knew quite a
bit about the business and knew it would pay off if handled
right. Said he was going to ride down to Tumble and see
if there might be an opening there. Contacted Lerner and
got the lowdown about Echo. They got together and he
opened up his place, the Diehard. 'Pears to be making a
go of it. Figure he will, all right; he's an up and coming
gent."

"His place in Echo was certainly catching on," Slade
observed. The sheriff nodded agreement.

Slade glanced out the window at the low-lying sun and rose to his feet.

"I'm going to take a walk," he announced. "If Mary shows up, tell her I'll be back shortly."

"Okay," said Crane. "But watch your step. Doc, the coroner, would like to hold an inquest on those carcasses in a couple of hours, if you can spare the time."

"Guess I can," Slade conceded. "Be seeing you."

For some time he wandered about aimlessly. He passed the noisy and bustling railroad yards but did not enter. He did pause at the rowdy Hog Wallow saloon for a few words with corpulent Cruikshanks, the owner, then continued his stroll, gradually working his way to the south edge of town, from where he would have a good view of the sunset.

As he walked, he continually scanned the brush-grown crest of the canyon east wall. That clifftop had developed into an unpleasant experience in the course of a previous visit to Sanderson.

So he was ready when he glimpsed a sudden flash as of sunlight reflecting from shifted metal and hurled himself sideways and down even as a gun blazed from the crest. The slug yelled over his prostrate form.

For tense moments he lay motionless, risking the life-and-death gamble that the drygulcher, thinking him done for, wouldn't fire again.

The moments dragged past with nothing happening, then a head pushed cautiously through the brush at the cliff edge and peered down.

Prone on the ground, Slade drew and shot, and again, and again. The head vanished from sight, but the brush was wildly agitated, as from something thrashing about. Then the body of a man bulged through the growth, rolled over the lip of the cliff and hurtled down to strike the rocks hundreds of feet below with a frightful thud.

For more moments Slade lay motionless, his eyes never leaving the clifftop. But there was no more movement of the growth. Evidently the devil had been alone. Still watchful, he stood up and walked to where the drygulcher's body lay.

It was not a pretty sight. The face had been smashed and sliced until it was difficult to recognize it as being human.

Now men were running from various directions, shouting. Soon they were close.

"Why, it's Mr. Slade!" somebody exclaimed. "What happened, Mr. Slade?"

"Looks like the gent over there, what's left of him, fell off the cliff," Slade replied. "Take a look."

They did take a look, indulging in some vivid profanity. The man who had recognized Slade chuckled.

"Yep. He fell over, all right. You all right, Mr. Slade?" The crowd appeared to regard the passage as the best of jokes.

"Hope some more of the same brand fall off a cliff," somebody else chortled delightedly. "What shall we do with the carcass, Mr. Slade?"

"Pack it to the sheriff's office," Slade replied. "And please, somebody go to the Branding Pen and tell the sheriff to meet me at the office."

A couple of the crowd hurried off to take care of the chore. Four others seized the body by the arms and legs and headed for the office. Slade lingered a moment.

"Suppose some of you go up top and locate his horse," he suggested to the gathering. "Strip off the rig and put the critter in the sheriff's stable."

"Right away, Mr. Slade," was the immediate compliance.

When they reached the office, they found not only the sheriff but Mary Merril also. She shook her head resignedly.

"Out of my sight for two hours and you're in trouble!"

"Must you blame me because a gent takes a notion to fall off a cliff?" Slade protested.

The sally was greeted with uproarious laughter by the gathering.

After a little, Crane shooed the crowd out and locked the door. He and Slade examined the body.

"No bullet wounds I can see," he remarked.

"I think my second shot caught him between the eyes, and his head and face are too crushed for the wound to show," Slade explained.

"So I reckon Doc Cooper and his jury will have to bring in a verdict of accidental death," the sheriff commented. "You *thought* your bullet struck him, but you couldn't swear to it."

"Guess that's right," Slade was forced to admit.

"More money," Crane remarked as he emptied the drygulcher's pockets. "Wonder how the devil he figured he would get a shot at you from the clifftop?"

"Evidently they have been keeping tabs on my movements and knew I have a habit of viewing the sunset from the south edge of town and would walk by the cliff," Slade replied. "But they never seem to learn that the gun will reflect sunlight as they shift it to line sights. That works in my favor."

"Uh-huh, what nobody without your eyes would notice," grunted the sheriff.

"Anyhow, it was clumsily handled and didn't work, and that's all that counts," Slade said. "But darn 'em, they made me miss the sunset," he added, gazing out at the deepening dusk.

"Plenty more sunsets," Crane predicted cheerfully. "Right now I'm more interested in a coupla snorts. How about it?"

"Just a minute," Slade said. "Here comes Doc Cooper and his coroner's jury to hold an inquest. Won't take long."

It didn't. The three outlaws slain outside of Echo met their death at the hands of law-enforcement officers in the performance of their duty. The other evidently committed suicide by jumping off a cliff; the community didn't lose anything. Court adjourned, the undertaker took over and the bodies were carted to Sanderson's already flourishing Boot Hill. Slade and his companions headed for the Branding Pen and their belated dinner.

The killing of the drygulcher was being discussed in the Branding Pen, with considerable conjecture as to what part Slade might have played in the incident. But because there appeared to be uncertainty as to whether he was involved in it at all, their dinner was not uninterrupted. For which all was duly thankful.

After Slade and the sheriff had enjoyed a leisurely after-dinner smoke, Mary said, "I want to dance! All right, Walt, you promised." Slade knew better than to argue and led her to the floor.

They had done three numbers and had paused at the table to catch their breath, the last being a fast one, when Westbrook Lerner came hurrying in, powdered with dust but with his eyes snapping. He hurried to the table. Mary proceeded to take the wind out of his sails.

"Hello, Mr. Lerner," she said. "Walt and Uncle Tom figured out the best route for the carts to follow from Sanderson to Echo."

Lerner gulped and sputtered. "If you don't beat all!" he exclaimed. "You're bad as Walt when it comes to getting the jump on everybody and having everything lined up in advance. I had a nice big argument to convince you that switching from Tumble to Echo would be to your advantage. Thought you'd take it for granted I'd discuss the matter with you."

"A woman should never take anything for granted, Mr. Lerner," Mary replied. "Suppose you have a list of what you will need."

"Right here," Lerner said, fishing it from his pocket and handing it to her. She glanced over it rapidly, nodded.

"I'll take it over to the boys at the bar," she said. "Most of them are there, including Saxon. A few are missing. I notice a few of the dance-floor girls are also missing. Oh, well, I suppose they like to look at the stars."

"Viewed from the proper position they must be worth looking at," remarked the sheriff, gazing at the ceiling.

"And a little *latigo* tightening would become you," Mary told him as she headed for the bar. She was back after a short conversation with Clay Saxon, the head carter.

"Okay, tomorrow we load and the next morning we roll to Echo," she said. "And now I wish to visit the Hog Wallow and have a little talk with that nice Mr. Cruikshanks who owns it."

"That rowdy rumhole!" groaned the sheriff. "Oh, well, guess I can bear up under the strain, but I never expect to be the same afterward."

"Might be an improvement," Mary retorted. "Let's go!"

"Guess I might as well toddle along, too," said Lerner. "Suppose I can tie onto something to eat there."

"Do have to credit them with putting out good chuck," Crane told him. "And being in *El Halcón*'s company won't hurt."

Waving to Hardrock and the whooping carters, they departed and made their way to the Hog Wallow across from the railroad yards, which was even more crowded

34

and boisterous than the Branding Pen, which was saying plenty.

At the bar were the missing carters, each with a Branding Pen dance-floor girl beside him. Hardrock did not mind his girls fraternizing with the customers, but he demanded that they be absolutely square-shooting; the carters had nothing to worry about.

The carters waved, the girls giggled self-consciously. Slade and Mary both smiled and put them at their ease.

Also at the bar, talking with the portly, rubicund Cruikshanks was Vince Rader, the Diehard owner.

"Getting some pointers on how an up-and-coming place is run," guessed Lerner. The sheriff snorted. Slade regarded the Echo saloonkeeper with greater interest.

Cruikshanks disengaged himself from Rader, who smiled and nodded, waddled across the room to greet them, and in person conducted them to a table near the dance floor, beckoning a waiter.

"Well, well! Miss Mary," he rumbled. "So you brought 'em back to old Jonathan. Plumb obliged to you."

"Oh, they didn't need much urging," Mary replied. "They like it here, as I do. Of course Uncle Tom had to cut loose a growl or two. But that's habitual with him. If he was in Heaven sitting on a mossy log, he'd find something to complain about."

"Well, I ain't complainin' about this helpin' of redeye," said Crane, sampling his glass. "It's prime."

Lerner's hankering for food was bountifully taken care of, and he also found nothing to complain of. The kitchen door opened a crack and the cook and his helpers bowed to *El Halcón*, who sauntered across to the kitchen and conversed with them in Spanish and left them greatly pleased.

"He never forgets the little people," Lerner murmured.

"Really big men don't," Mary said.

"And he's big, in every sense of the word," Lerner nodded, as did the Hog Wallow owner.

"Sit down and keep us company for a while, Uncle Jonathan," Mary invited.

"Don't mind if I do," Cruikshanks accepted, easing his bulk into a chair that creaked and swayed under his weight. "Been standing up all evening. See you know Mr. Rader from Echo. Been talking with him for quite a while. Being new to the section, he asked a lot of questions about conditions and the best way to handle difficulties. Strikes me as a gent who'll make out all right. What do you think, Mr. Slade?"

"I'd say he'll do well at anything to which he turns his hand," *El Halcón* replied. Mary shot him a quick look, a little pucker between her slender black brows.

The carters and their girls had quietly slipped out. A few minutes later, Vince Rader emulated their example, nodding and smiling as he passed the table. Slade's thoughtful eyes followed him to the swinging doors. Mary regarded Slade. Then she glanced at the clock.

"Thank you for everything, Uncle Jonathan," she said. "It is really late and we must be going. Work tomorrow."

"I'll see to it that the loading starts on time, Miss Mary," Lerner offered. "You sleep as long as you wish."

The sheriff chuckled over his glass. Mary shot him a disdainful look. He lingered in converse with Lerner for a moment or two. Slade and Mary walked under the stars to the hotel. The old desk clerk snored gently as they mounted the stairs together.

Slade arose around noon, and after a belated **SIX** breakfast, repaired to the sheriff's office, where he found Crane smoking the pipe of peace and gazing out the window at the golden sunglow.

"Well, now what?" he asked, blowing out a cloud of tobacco smoke.

"Now we'll try and figure a way to outconnive our owl-hoot *amigos*," the Ranger replied. "Got any suggestions?"

"Not a darn one," snorted the sheriff. "How about you?"

"I'm still groping," Slade said. "As you said, there are so many darn things that fill the bill. One thing I plan to do is visit Charley, the bank president, and learn what he knows. He's been a help to us before."

"That's a notion," Crane agreed. "Charley is all right and always glad to work with us. Going now?"

"Might as well," Slade decided. "Nothing to be gained by putting it off. Be seeing you soon."

Slade had no difficulty obtaining an interview with the president. Old friends, they shook hands warmly.

"And what's on your mind, Walt?" the banker asked, after sending for coffee and a drink. "Something bothering you?"

Slade came to the point without delay. "Charley," he said, "do you know of any money shipment arriving here that might be of interest to an outlaw bunch?"

The president pondered, glanced over some papers on his desk.

"There is only one thing I can think of," he finally said. "There's a quite large money shipment coming in from Laredo on the westbound El Paso Flyer that gets here about eleven o'clock tonight. It will be deposited with us to the credit of a man in the new town of Echo who I understand is opening up a place in Echo. Doubtless needs the money to complete his building, and so forth."

"And the man?" Slade asked.

"Fellow named Frederick Norton. Fred Norton I believe he calls himself. Does it help you any?"

"It may help me a good deal," Slade told him. "Thanks, Charley, very much. You are always cooperative."

37

"Got to keep on the good side of the—law," the banker smiled. "Take care of yourself, Walt."

Leaving the bank, Slade did not at once return to the sheriff's office. Instead, he wandered about in the sunshine for quite a while, thinking and mapping a course of action. He felt that what he learned from the banker could be highly important, possibly providing the opportunity he sorely needed. Fred Norton, who was opening up the Wallop saloon in Echo. Doubtless he did need money with which to get his place in running order. He returned to the office and informed Sheriff Crane of what he learned from the president.

"And you figure the devils might make a try for that dinero?" Crane asked.

"I think it not beyond the realm of the possible," *El Halcón* answered. "The money will be in the express-car safe and will be handed to the bank representative who will be on hand to receive it. There'll be a guard with him, of course, but that wouldn't deter them if they really mean business. So I want you and the deputies to keep an eye on things. Don't make it obvious, and don't take chances. It's a killer bunch."

"You're darn right," growled Crane. "And what do you plan to do?"

"Later I plan to take a little ride," Slade answered.

The sheriff looked expectant, but the Ranger did not elaborate, and Crane asked no questions. He knew very well that *El Halcón* would talk when he was ready to, and not before.

"Okay," he said. "Just take care of yourself. We'll handle things at this end."

Visiting the cart station, Slade had a few words with Mary Merril and Lerner, leaving both looking anxious. However, both knew better than to try and dissuade him when he had something in mind.

"Expect I'll see you both before the carts roll," he told them. "I'll be riding before dark."

He did ride, less than an hour before sunset. He rode north by east. To all appearances, he was heading for Echo. Often before the sun set, he gazed back the way he had come, marveling at the tremendous vista spread before his eyes. West of Sanderson, the far-flung outposts of the Big Bend, and those of the trans-Pecos area—the

Bullis Gap Range, the Haymond Mountains, the Pena Blancas, the Woods Hollow Mountains, and the craggy Glass Mountains.

Seen or unseen, they were there, grim, immutable, flinging their challenge to the sunset glory of the heavens. Of the eternities, they. Slade rode on, north by east.

But as the darkness of the night closed down, he changed his course to almost due south, but steadily veering eastward though slightly. Without drawing rein he reached the east-west river trail and followed its more easterly course. He spoke to his horse.

"The little slips, Shadow, the little slips. Always they make them," he said. "And almost always to our advantage. I'm sure about this one. Tell you more later."

Shadow snorted resignedly and ambled on. Having followed this route more than once in the past, he doubtless knew his master's destination was the junction of the Tumble short-line with the east-west line over which the El Paso Flyer ran.

Now Slade rode watchful and alert, for he was no great distance from the junction, where he believed the attempt, were one made, would take place. Just how, he didn't know. On the occasion of a former visit to the section, the El Paso Flyer express car was robbed at the junction. There was a slow order past the junction, and when the Flyer rounded the curve to the east, the engineer saw a man swinging a stop-sign signal with a red lantern. He acknowledged the signal and brought his long train to a halt. The robbers took over the engine, cleaned the express-car safe after shooting the express messenger.

Slade was confident that procedure would not be tried a second time, for now the train crews were very much on the alert when passing the junction at night, the express messenger barricaded in his car. If an attempt was made, it would be something novel and unexpected.

Over to one side was a shack that housed a telegraph instrument, but no operator on duty during the night hours. And running to join the east-west line was a spur on which sometimes freight cars loaded with materials stood, though seldom.

A moon was rising in the east, flooding the scene with silvery light, but because there was a stand of chaparral growth paralleling the railroad and encroaching on the trail, Slade was confident his approach would not be spotted, especially coming from the west, the last direction from which anybody was likely to come. Also, the robbers, were they really on the job, would doubtless be concentrating on the east and the expected Flyer. He quickened Shadow's pace a little, for now he was not far from the junction and would soon be in a position to view anything going on there. And the Flyer would be due very shortly. He rounded a shallow curve, hugging the growth, and the junction and its environs lay before him.

There was no engine standing on the Tumble main line, which would be the case were there passengers or freight for Tumble on the local that would follow the Flyer. All was dark in the shack. Looked like the outlaws, were there any around, had a clear field for whatever they had in mind. There was a boxcar standing on the spur that led to the east-west main line. He slowed Shadow a little.

Suddenly to his remarkably keen ears came a sound, a click-clicking as of metal working on metal. What the devil!

His eyes swept the terrain, centered on the boxcar. Blazes! The darn thing was moving! Very slowly, but moving. Moving down the spur to the east-west main line!

And now he recognized that mysterious clicking for what it was. Somebody was manipulating a manual car mover, nudging the boxcar toward the main line. With the spur derailer flipped over, the boxcar would be shoved onto the main line right in front of the Flyer! And the resulting smashup would provide the outlaws all the opportunity they would need to achieve their evil ends.

And now he saw there were three men grouped behind the car, one working the lever of the car mover. Slade's voice rang out:

"Trail, Shadow, trail!"

Instantly the great horse lunged forward, spurning the earth with his hoofs. The outlaws heard the pound of his flying irons and whirled around. A gun flashed, and another, the bullets whining past the Ranger.

And the boxcar had split the switch and was leaning over the westbound main line!

Whipping his high-power Winchester from the saddle boot, Slade opened fire. One of the outlaws spun sideways and fell. The other two shot as fast as they could squeeze

40

trigger, their slugs fanning Slade's face, one ripping the sleeve of his shirt, just graining the flesh. He shifted the Winchester muzzle a trifle. The big rifle gushed flame and smoke, and another robber fell. The one remaining dashed around the rear end of the boxcar. Fast hoofs beat southward.

Slade did not pursue; he had other matters urgently in need of attention. For from the east, beyond the curve, sounded a mellow whistle note. The Flyer was on the rail!

"Trail, Shadow, trail!" he shouted. Shadow increased his already flying speed. Slade sent him as far as he dared, swerved him onto the tracks, and jerked him to a halt.

Around the curve roared the Flyer. Slade whipped off his hat and swung it frantically back and forth. The engineer, seeing that wildly waving mounted figure, knew something was terribly wrong. He jammed the throttle shut, slammed on the brakes. Peering ahead, he saw the boxcar overhanging the track.

Back came the reverse bar, to the front of the quadrant. The throttle was jerked wide open. The stack thundered. The great drive wheels, spinning in reverse, planed off ribbons of steel from the rails. With brake and throttle, the engineer fought to save his train.

Too late! With a terrific crash the Flyer sideswiped the boxcar. The engine was derailed and went thudding and careening over the ties, the pilot splintered, the brake rigging torn free, steam bellowing from the broken pipes.

The locomotive ground to a halt, leaning dangerously, but on its wheels. The baggage and express cars also were derailed, but like the engine, stayed erect.

Shadow, who had jumped in the clear just in time, blew and snorted disgustedly. Slade drew a deep breath as he replaced his hat. Could have been a lot worse. Was nothing to what would have happened had the boxcar been out on the main line.

The fireman and engineer climbed out of the cab and dropped to the ground, spewing profanity. Both were bruised, slightly burned, with a few minor cuts.

Slade rode to meet the hogger and the tallowpot—railroad parlance for engineer and fireman.

"What the blinkin' blue blazes," the former began. "Hey! It's Mr. Slade, Sheriff Crane's special deputy. What did happen, Mr. Slade? How'd that thing get shoved down the spur that way?"

Slade told them, briefly. They stared at him, stared at the demolished boxcar.

"And if that thing had been shoved clear out onto the line, we'd have hit it head on, the engine would have been turned over, and maybe about half the coaches," the engineer said slowly, his face grim. "Looks like we're mighty beholden to you, Mr. Slade."

El Halcón changed the subject as the blue-clad conductor, with whom he was also acquainted, came hurrying from the coaches, which were pandemonium personified, the terrified passengers screaming and yelling and cursing.

"First thing we'll break open that shack—a telegraph instrument in there—and notify Sanderson," he told the conductor. "Then I'll talk to you, Chuck."

He dismounted, dropped the split reins to the ground, and led the way to the shack.

"Darn thing's locked," the conductor growled.

"Stand back," Slade told him as he drew one of his Colts. A bullet from the big gun and the lock flew to pieces. Slade sat down at the table that accommodated the telegraph instrument, opened the key, and began sending. He got Sanderson, outlined briefly what had happened, and ordered the wreck train sent at once, and a string of coaches to shuttle the Flyer's passengers to Sanderson. In conclusion, he ordered that Sheriff Crane and Doc Cooper be located and sent along with the wreck train. He got his okay from Sanderson, closed the key, and they left the shack.

First thing, Slade flipped out Shadow's bit and loosened his cinches so the big horse could graze in comfort and drink from a nearby trickle of water.

"Everything eastbound is being held at Sanderson," he told the conductor. "You have a flag out to halt westbound traffic?"

"Yep, he's out," replied the con. "Local should be along any minute now."

Next Slade examined the injured passengers, discounted their hurts as of little consequence.

"Doc Cooper will patch them up on the way to Sander-

42

son," he said. "Nothing but a few bruises and a minor cut or two."

"But if it wasn't for him, you'd have a lot more to be patched up, those of you that were still alive," said the engineer.

Slade considered the statement something of an exaggeration but hardly saw fit to argue the point, although he was forced to endure a round of plaudits. He changed the subject by suggesting that the bodies of the slain outlaws be examined. The general consensus of opinion was that they were mean-looking devils and had gotten exactly what was coming to them. Slade thought them representative of their brand, perhaps a bit more intelligent than the average. One had been a former cowhand, the other had not.

Their horses were discovered, tethered nearby. The rigs were removed and they were turned loose to fend for themselves until picked up.

"And now, Chuck, if your kitchen is still functioning, I could use a cup of coffee," Slade told the conductor.

"Come right along, everything will be taken care of," that worthy instantly promised. He led the way to the diner, and soon Slade was plied with steaming coffee and tasty sandwiches.

"The wreck train boys are going to have quite a chore on their hands," the conductor, who was also partaking of coffee, remarked. "Nigh onto a hundred feet of track torn up and the engine in bad shape. Luckily there's a siding here and the wreck train can work from that. But I sure can't get over what could have happened, were it not for you. Get the shakes every time I think of it. The fireman and engineer would have sure for certain been killed, and mighty likely the baggagemaster and the express agent too, instead of just getting bruised a bit."

Slade was finishing a final cup of coffee and a cigarette when a whistle note sounded the arrival of the wreck train.

"Let's go," he said, and led the way outside.

The wreck train, backing up, was shunted onto the siding and eased down to where it too was partly blocked by the wrecked Flyer. Sheriff Crane and Doc Cooper dropped from the caboose, with them Mary Merril.

"When the yard whistles summoned the wreck train

crew we knew very well that you were mixed up in something down here, so of course I came along," the girl said to Slade. "All right, let's hear about it."

They heard, briefly, the conductor putting in a few words where he felt them due. Crane gave the dead outlaws a once-over, extracting considerable money from their pockets, but nothing else of significance.

"Figure the one that got away was the big he-wolf of the pack?" he asked.

"Frankly I couldn't say, but I've a notion he is," Slade answered. "The manner in which he reacted and grasped opportunity to escape, darting across the railroad into the brush on the far side, causes me to think he well might be."

"Didn't see what he looked like?"

Slade shook his head. "The light was not good, and I was sorta busy right then. All I can say is that he seemed sort of on the big side."

"Hmmm!" said the sheriff.

"Don't go sounding off," Slade warned. "Plenty of big men hereabouts." The sheriff snorted and changed the subject.

"Had a stall car hooked onto the coaches that are following the wreck train, to take care of your cayuse so you won't have to take that long night ride to town," he announced.

"That was considerate of you," Slade said.

"Oh, she was the one that thought of it first," Crane grunted, jerking his thumb toward Mary. "Guess she didn't want to be lonesome—the rest of the night." Slade smiled.

Mary made a face. "Saxon is rolling the carts in the morning," she said. "Mr. Lerner is going along to show him the best route. I'll get there some time."

Doc Cooper reported that Slade was right, no injuries of any consequence that wouldn't do with a little patching. And a little later the coaches, also backing up, arrived. The passengers were herded into them, Shadow into his stall car, the bodies into the caboose, and the trip to Sanderson began.

Without incident they reached the railroad town, where a special was waiting to accommodate those whose destinations were points west of Sanderson.

Also waiting was a bank official and three armed guards

to transport the money from the express-car safe, which Slade and the sheriff had convoyed, to the bank. Both deputies were there and took care of the bodies. Slade stabled Shadow and everybody called it a night.

When Slade reached the office around noon, **SEVEN**
he found Sheriff Crane, always an early riser,
already there, contemplating with satisfaction the blanketed
bodies on the floor.

"Looks so much nicer with decorations," he said. "Well, wreck is cleaned up and trains are running on schedule again. Express company representative was in. Wanted to thank you for what you did. His company would have had to make good the loss, of course. And by the way, Vince Rader, the Diehard owner, was in the Branding Pen earlier. Looked tired in not too good temper. Didn't talk with Hardrock. Just had a couple of drinks and left."

"He's a busy man," Slade commented.

"Uh-huh, real busy, I figure," the sheriff remarked. "Well, how about some breakfast? Reckon you haven't eaten either."

"A notion," Slade agreed. "Let's go."

Meanwhile, railroad builders had descended on Tumble like a swarm of locusts. But, unlike the winged pests, they paid for what they ate and drank, which did not displease the Tumble business people.

Slade knew that for the first seven miles the road would meet with no difficulty, for it would be crossing Bob Kerr's Four K holding, and Kerr was one of his close friends. But the following eight miles, nearer ten by the route the road would follow, was different. The steel would have to cross two spreads, long east by west, narrow north by south, whose owners he gathered were not favorably disposed to the coming of the road.

Of course Eminent Domain could be invoked, but Jaggers Dunn did not like to invoke Eminent Domain were it possible not to, preferring to deal amicably with local people.

Well, it looked like it was up to him, Slade, to do something about it. What? At the moment he hadn't the slightest idea, but he was confident that he would eventually be able to surmount the difficulty; he always was. He put the matter out of his mind for the present and concentrated on the bountiful breakfast the old Mexican cook had provided.

While they were eating, Mary bounced in, declaring she was starved.

"Finally get some sleep?" the sheriff asked.

"I did," the big-eyed girl replied. "And no snide comments from the gallery!"

The sheriff chuckled and refrained from comment, snide or otherwise.

"Your carts rolled on time," he said a little later. "The boys all seemed happy."

"And I think I'll follow them," Mary replied. "I'd like to be in Echo to check the lists of what will be needed for the next shipment. Mr. Lerner is fixing up a place for me to sleep."

"Hmmm!" said the sheriff. "Reckon you'd better go along, Walt."

"Frankly I think I shall," Slade said. "It's a lonely ride."

"And with all sorts of critters traipsin' in from all over," Crane added. "A gal has no business taking that ride alone."

An hour later they set out, under a sun-washed sky as blue as Mary's eyes, Slade mounted on Shadow, the girl on Rojo, her big red-sorrel.

"And what would have been a chore is instead a pleasure," she murmured, reining Rojo in a little closer.

"Yes?"

"Yes, and you know it, all too well."

Slade was silent. He was instinctively watchful as they rode, although he knew they had nothing to fear on the open prairie. Not mounted on such horses as Shadow and Rojo, plus his long-range Winchester.

When they reached the hills surrounding the great cup it would be different. However, it was highly unlikely that anybody would anticipate his riding to Echo, and though he redoubled his caution when they approached the hills, he was not particularly apprehensive.

His deductions proved correct. They mounted the slope, crossed the crest to the lip of the farther sag without incident.

The scene that lay before them was quite different than on the occasion of Slade's first visit. Now instead of only three, there were nearly a dozen drilling derricks rising,

47

walking beams jigging, drill bits thudding. There were more houses. And the big shack that accommodated the Diehard saloon appeared to be completed, at least on the outside.

Satisfied everything was under control, they rode down the sag and across the field. This time quite a few of the workers called greetings, which they acknowledged. But they did not draw rein until they reached Lerner's place on the far side of the field. The oil magnate came hurrying out to meet them.

"This is fine!" he exclaimed. "Light off and come in; just in time for dinner."

He let out a whoop and the stable keeper, who had been introduced to Shadow before, came hustling and led the cayuses to their stalls, leaving the pouches and Slade's rifle behind. Lerner led the way into the house. With a chuckle he waved his hand to the stairs to the second floor.

"The boys obeyed orders and stirred their stumps," he said. "Come on up and take a look."

When they reached the second floor, they found it now boasted two bedrooms, furnished, even to wash bowls.

"Which is whose?" Mary asked with a giggle.

"You can fight that out between you," Lerner replied. "I don't aim to get embroiled. There's plenty of running water if you want to wash up. Hear that pump clanking? It's piping from the big spring over by the foot of the slope. No hot water yet, except what we heat on the stove, but I expect to have that before long."

"Who wants hot water!" Mary retorted cheerfully. "Cold is just as wet, and that's what counts. Walt, dear, fetch my pouches, please, and I'll make myself presentable for you. And later I think I'd like to do the town."

"Here we go again!" Slade sighed as he went down to attend to the chore.

"Don't fuss," Mary admonished. "You like it just as I do, and you know it." Slade didn't argue the point. Arguing with Miss Merril got you exactly nowhere, which he very well knew. He brought his own pouches and his rifle along and proceeded to enjoy a good wash.

He and Lerner were sitting in the office, talking and smoking, when Mary trotted down the stairs.

"Well, how do I look?" she asked. Slade regarded her costume with a critical eye.

"Like an escapee from a dance floor," was his verdict.

"That's just the way I want to look," she enthused. "What do you think, Mr. Lerner?"

"That you would grace any dance floor, or anyplace off one, for that matter," was the gallant reply. Mary dropped him a curtsey.

"I'm hungry," she said.

"Just the right way to be," said Lerner. "For here's Juan to announce your dinner is ready. You'll have to eat off a table in the kitchen. Haven't gotten around to a dining room yet."

"I like kitchens," Mary replied. "And cooks too," she added, giving the old fellow a dazzling smile that caused him to glow with pleasure.

When they sat down to table, Mary thought the repast he dished up was worth a dozen smiles, and told him so.

By the time they finished their meal, it was full dark and Echo was beginning to hum as the workers knocked off for the day. Soon the hum would louden to a boom town's nightly roar. Slade felt his pulses quicken. For, reprehensible fact, he liked such nights in such an environment. And he knew his companions did too.

"Your carters will be at the Diehard," Lerner remarked to Mary. "They took to the place first off."

"And I want to go there, too, after a while," the girl said. "With my boys there it will be lively."

"And there will be plenty other of the same brand," Lerner said. "Never a dull moment in the Diehard.

"And my boys are sure grateful for the casings and other materials your carts brought," he added. "They're yelping for more and are talking about a bonus for fast delivery."

"Never mind the bonus," Mary said. "I'm perfectly satisfied with the deal you made with them for me. Tell them they'll get delivery as fast as is possible. We'll finish the unloading tomorrow and roll the empties back to Sanderson. Suppose you have a list of what is needed most."

"In my desk," Lerner replied. "As soon as you check it, I'll hand it to Saxon and he'll get busy right away."

"Okay," Mary said. "And now let's forget business for

49

the rest of the night and just enjoy ourselves for a change. What do you say, Walt?"

"The music of your voice supplies me with all the enjoyment I need," Slade replied.

"Whenever he is away for a while, he comes back saying pretty things," Mary sighed. "I wonder who teaches him them. If I can find out, she'll learn I have fingernails."

"No doubt as to that," Slade said, with a reminiscent twitch of his shoulders.

"And that will be plenty from you," Mary retorted. "Fetch the list, Uncle Westbrook, and I'll check it, and then the Diehard."

"Now she's adopted me as an avuncular relative," chuckled Lerner. "I feel complimented."

Checking the list didn't take long. Then they headed for the Diehard, walking the busy and lighted streets with the glitter of the stars spangling the blue-black sky.

The Diehard was lively, all right, with evidence of the fact apparent when they were still a block away. When they entered, the carters, present in a body, let out a joyous whoop and demands that they have a drink.

"No gainsaying them if we wish to have any peace," Slade accepted.

Vince Rader, the owner, came hurrying to greet them and escort them to a table. He beckoned a waiter.

"Everything on the house, of course," he said. "Have to keep on the good side of the law, and the ladies. And seeing that Mr. Lerner so generously donated the land on which my building stands, I'd be a fine one if I allowed him to spend money here."

"Would be a good investment," Lerner said. He and Slade had drinks. Mary accepted a small glass of wine.

Looking the room over, Slade was rather surprised to see a couple of cowhands at the bar, mingling with the carters, some of whom they evidently knew, having doubtless met them in Tumble or Sanderson. He also noted that some oil field workers were regarding the rannies a trifle askance. However, they made no inimical moves or gestures.

Just the same, Slade felt that the situation was fraught with potential trouble, and kept it in mind.

"I want to dance," Mary said. "Come on, Walt." They moved onto the crowded floor, followed by admiring glances. Several numbers, some of them fast, before they returned to their chairs for a breather.

"You had everybody watching you," said Lerner. "Guess they got a chance to see what real dancing is."

"As Uncle Tom Crane would say, they ain't seen nothin' yet," Mary declared. She flounced out of her chair and trotted across the room to hold converse with the orchestra leader, whose face was abruptly wreathed in smiles. He seized a guitar and waved it insinuatingly at Slade.

"You're elected," chuckled Lerner.

"Yes, if I expect to have any peace the rest of the evening." Rising, he made his way to the platform. The leader brandished the guitar like a war club and shouted, *"Señoritas* and *Señores,* the great treat is for us due. *Capitán* will sing!"

The carters, who knew what to expect, gave vent to happy yelps. Slade accepted the guitar, smiled the white smile of *El Halcón,* and sang.

Of the mighty Empire of the Southwest he sang, of its turbulent past, its mighty future. Of the men and women who made and were making the West. Of its beauty and its terror, its sunny plains of summer, its icy mountains of winter. Of the rangeland he sang, the thundering herds, the glinting horns, the gray horror of the stampede, with death in frightful form beneath the churning hoofs. Of the campfire and the stars. And of the imprisoned sunshine, the "black gold," gushing from the abysmal depths of the earth to spin the wheels of progress.

And as his golden baritone-bass pealed and thundered through the room, before the eyes of his entranced hearers it all passed in review, the saga of the West, made real by the magic of a great voice.

Turning to the dance floor, he flashed another smile and,

> "Ambition breaks like falling rain,
> Glory's a vain endeavor.
> The stars may fall, the sun grow dark,
> But love abideth ever!"

Amid salvos of applause that shook the rafters, he returned the guitar to the leader, who bowed low to *El Halcón* and walked back to his table.

There were tears on Mary Merril's dark lashes, but she dashed them away and managed a tremulous smile.

Rader paused beside them. "Thank you, Mr. **EIGHT** Slade, thank you very much. You have a wonderful voice. May your carter boys send over another round of drinks? They would very much like to."

"Thank you, I'll settle for coffee this time," Slade replied.

"Short for me," said Lerner.

"And I would like a small glass of wine," Mary said.

They raised glasses and cup to the carters, who whooped joyously, emptied theirs and hammered for refills.

The two cowhands were still at the bar but were beginning to look a mite the worse for wear. Slade watched them closely.

Lerner asked Mary to dance and they moved to the floor. Slade sat sipping his coffee and watching the cowhands.

A few moments later they weaved through the swinging doors. Playing a hunch, Slade got up and sauntered after them, keeping several paces to the rear of the inebriated pair, who walked unsteadily and slowly, heading straight across town.

Back of Fred Norton's Wallop saloon was a narrow alley, little more than a crack between the two rows of buildings. The pair started past the dark mouth.

From the alley barged two men dressed in oil worker's clothes. They closed in behind the two punchers.

Just in time, Slade saw the gleam of the raised knife. He whipped out his Colts and shot with both hands.

The knife flew through the air. The wielder gave a yelp of pain and whirled to face Slade, drawing with his left hand. His companion followed suit.

Back and forth gushed the orange flashes. Bullets whizzed past the ducking, dodging, slithering Ranger. Almost as suddenly as it began, the burst of gunfire stilled. Slade peered through the powder fog at the two motionless forms on the board sidewalk. The two cowboys were sagging against the building wall, looking dazed, but undoubtedly quite a bit sobered by the grim episode.

The racket in the Wallop, which had stilled for a moment, burst forth afresh. The cowhands who had been drinking there came boiling through the swinging doors, yelling and questioning.

"Quiet!" Slade thundered. "Everything is under control. Somebody fetch a lamp or a lantern."

"What happened, Mr. Slade?" somebody who recognized him called.

"I'll tell you what happened," replied one of the decidedly sobered punchers from the Diehard. "Those two devils on the ground there tried to knife us in the back. Mr. Slade kept them from doing it."

"A couple of blasted oil workers," said a voice. An ominous growl went up from the cowhands.

Slade decided to risk a gamble in hope of preventing an explosion of real violence, which was in the making, oil workers now joining the group.

"Bring that lamp here," he ordered the man who had fetched one. He deftly turned out the pockets of the dead killers, breathing relief as he bared the linty seams.

"Take a look and tell me what you see in the seams," he directed the Wallop cowhands, who bent close.

"Dust," one said, "gray dust. Looks like desert dust— there's a stretch of desert over to the west of here."

Slade spoke, slowly and impressively. "And if this pair were oil field workers, wouldn't that dust be dark and greasy?"

"Why—why, guess it would," conceded the cowhand. "What does it mean, Mr. Slade?"

"It means, just as I said of those hellions who tried to drygulch Sheriff Crane and myself, who dressed like cowhands and were not, that it was a deliberate attempt to stir up trouble between the spread owners and the oil field and the railroad. This pair were not oil field workers, and very likely never were. Same old story, set two outfits of honest men on the prod against each other, blaming each other for everything off-color that happens, giving the owlhoots a free hand to operate. Beginning to understand?"

"Guess we are," admitted the cowhand. His companions and the oil workers nodded agreement. The two groups began mingling.

Slade experienced a surge of satisfaction. He had won his gamble, so far as the hands and the oil workers were concerned. Now if he could just manage to bring a couple of stubborn ranch owners down off their high horse, he would have the situation really under control and would be able to concentrate on the chore he was sent into the section to perform, the apprehension of the vicious outlaw bunch that was plaguing the section, and putting an end to their nefarious activities.

However, he felt he hadn't done too bad, so far, although he still didn't have a really definite idea as to who was the head of the bunch.

Lerner and Mary Merril appeared, hurriedly, the carters trailing after them and ready for business did Slade require assistance. Mary had her hand in the rather large pocket of her short dancing skirt and Slade knew in that hand was a gun, very likely at full cock.

"We heard the shooting, of course, and followed the crowd," Lerner explained. "Did those two devils make a try for you? Just what did happen?"

He was told, volubly, from various sources. Lerner looked serious, but pleased.

"Looks like you've managed to get the boys together," he murmured, regarding the merging groups. "Well, that helps a lot."

"Out of sight and into trouble," sighed Mary. "I'm hungry!"

Slade collected the money the dead outlaws' pockets had disgorged, a considerable sum. He divided it into two heaps, the smaller of which he handed to the two cowboys who had been the focus of the trouble.

"To make up for the scare you got," he said. Which brought forth delighted grins from the recipients.

"The rest goes to the county treasury," he added, stowing it away.

"Norton has his kitchen going at last, so I reckon we might as well give the Wallop a whirl for a snack," Lerner said. "The carters are already in there. Hear 'em? I'll have the bodies covered and pack 'em to the sheriff's office tomorrow."

"Thanks," Slade said. "That will help."

When they entered the Wallop, greeted by whoops from carters, cowhands, and oil workers, Slade glanced around and failed to see Fred Norton, the owner.

"Went riding early in the afternoon," the waiter who

showed them to a table and took their order said. "He does a lot of riding. Wouldn't be surprised if he once had something to do with the cow business. He sets a horse like a cowhand. Everything on the house, Mr. Slade, that's Mr. Norton's orders, as I reckon Mr. Lerner knows."

Saxon, the head carter, caught Mary's eye. She nodded, and a little later Saxon rounded up his men and they departed to sleep in the enclosed shed Lerner had erected for their convenience.

The snack was dispatched mostly in silence, for everybody was getting just a mite weary. The waiter bobbed and grinned over the tip Slade slipped into his hand.

"Come again, folks, please, and soon," he begged.

"And now," Mary said as they headed for Lerner's domicile, "I'm ready to call it a night. Escort me upstairs, Walt."

He did.

Despite their hilarious night, the carters had their vehicles unloaded and ready to roll by midmorning. Saxon had the money received for the shipment stashed in his saddle pouch, and he rode with a rifle balanced across the saddle in front of him; the head carter was taking no chances. Slade, with Mary beside him, accompanied the train, for he was anxious to get in touch with Sheriff Crane. The bodies of the outlaws were already on their way to the sheriff's office.

Saxon did not have occasion to use his rifle, and without incident they reached Sanderson shortly before sunset. The carts were lined up in loading position. He and Mary went over the list of materials needed, while the carters descended on the Branding Pen in search of food and other refreshment. Mary went to her room to freshen up a bit and Slade headed for the sheriff's office.

"Much obliged for the decorations you sent me," old Tom said when he entered. "My floor looks nice and cosy again. Let's have the details of what took place. The boys who packed in the carcasses handed out a rather sketchy account, but I reckon there was more to it than they said."

Slade did so, briefly. Crane chuckled with pleasure when he learned of how Slade had gotten the cowhands and the oil field workers together.

"Yes, that helps a lot," he said. "Now all you have to do is hold a little palaver with those ringy old owner coots and convince them of the error of their ways."

"Sounds plumb simple, the way you put it," Slade smiled. "Well, we'll see. First off we'll try and do a little anticipating and try to figure where the hellions will strike next."

"And you think they'll make a try for something soon?"

"I do," Slade replied. "The head sidewinder must keep his devils well supplied with spending money. Besides, I've a notion a mite of morale boosting is in order. He's suffered quite a few losses and the others may be getting a bit jumpy in consequence. Also, losing out on the Flyer money must have hurt and he'll be out to even the score. So we'll do the best we can to hit him again where it hurts. What he may have in mind? Right now I haven't the vaguest idea. We'll just have to sit tight for the moment and hope something breaks for us."

Until past full dark they discussed the problem, conning over possibilities, of which there were too darn many, endeavoring to pinpoint something that might be intriguing to an outlaw bunch, with no satisfactory result.

"Oh, to heck with it, let's go eat," Crane finally said.

"About that time," Slade agreed.

The night passed without incident. The carters put on their usual antics, but otherwise everything was peaceful enough.

The next day Slade wandered about the town thinking, pondering the problem that faced him, hoping Fate would give him a break. Fate was going to do just that.

For a while he watched the loading of the carts, Mary shaking her curly head over the list of desired materials.

"Can't handle anything like all of it," she said. "Looks like I'll be investing in more carts."

"You're sure on the way to being a rich woman," Slade replied.

"Put not your faith in material things," she slightly misquoted. "Okay, dear, see you at dinner. Can't spare any more time right now."

Slade continued his stroll. Around late afternoon he visited the sheriff's office.

"Well," Crane said, "old Gird Blake who owns the

Square and Circle spread north of Bob Kerr's Four K came bellerin' in while you were out. He's one of those two ringy old coots that's opposing the oil field and the railroad. He said he lost better'n a hundred prime beef critters last night. Said he and his hands trailed the critters straight toward the river ford south of Tumble. But lost the trail on the heavy grass, although they did manage to follow the cuts made by the horses' irons for a bit farther before they lost them, too. Said there wasn't any doubt that they were headed for that ford and would pass close to Tumble, but that when something like that happened, those blankety-blanks in Tumble look the other way. He believes it."

"Which is exactly what the wideloopers want him to believe," Slade commented.

"What do you mean by that?" the sheriff asked.

"I mean that Blake played right into the rustler's hands," Slade replied. "It was handled very cleverly—sent the horses on a little farther than the cows, knowing that Blake would be able to spot the horses' iron marks for a while after he lost the cattle's prints. Those cows did not go past Tumble to the Tumble ford, not last night they didn't."

"Then where in blazes did they go?" groaned Crane.

Slade smiled and for some moments sat silent, then, "Tom, remember that range of low, brush-covered hills on Kerr's land, about three miles north of Tumble?"

"Why, yes, I do," answered the sheriff.

"Well," Slade said, "I'm ready to wager that right now Blake's cows are holed up in those hills and won't be moved from them until around midnight."

"If you say that's the way of it, I reckon it is," Crane replied. "What are we going to do about it?"

"Well," Slade said, "for one thing you and the deputies and I are going to take a little ride tonight."

"Going to root the critters outa the hills?"

Slade shook his head. "That would play right into the wideloopers' hands, as stupidly as Blake did. They'd spot us sure, and blow us from under our hats. I'll have a plan formulated by the time we ride. Will discuss that with you later. So far we have been largely on the defensive. This time we'll be carrying the fight to the enemy, and I consider an offensive is the best defense."

"Blake says he's going to have some of his hands stationed in Tumble to keep an eye on things," the sheriff remarked.

"The hands won't mind, and I guess he can afford it," was Slade's comment.

"And I guess we can afford a surroundin' at the Branding Pen," Crane said. "What do you say?"

"I'll take a chance," Slade agreed. "Mary will be there shortly; soon be dark. And after we eat, locate the deputies and line them up. We'll ride an hour or so after full dark."

They walked slowly through the deepening dusk, with Sanderson's riotous night life already getting under way. When they reached the Branding Pen, the carters were already assembled and whooping it up.

"I've a notion you've got the right of it," Crane said as he ordered a snort, Slade coffee to tide them over until Mary put in an appearance. "Yes, I think you have, and that the hellion is beginning to feel the money pinch. Losing out on those two good hauls, the Vanstaveren store and the Flyer express car, doesn't set well with his peace of mind, whoever the devil he is."

"And wet cows are a quick money turnover," Slade said. "Yes, he's all set to pull something, and it's up to us to throw a monkey wrench into his machinery, which I'm confident we are going to do. That is if he doesn't pull some sort of a rabbit out of the hat on us. There's always the chance that the shrewd devil has an ace in the hole. Well, we'll see."

Mary arrived shortly, hungry as usual. After she had finished her dinner, Slade broke the bad news.

"Oh, I expected it," she replied resignedly. "Two peaceful nights in a row were too much to hope for."

"We may be back before the carts are ready to roll," Slade told her. "Rather think we will. Otherwise I hope to see you in Echo before the empties head back this way." He glanced at the clock.

"Yes, we'd better be moving," he added.

"The deputies are waiting for us at the stable," Crane said.

They waved to Hardrock and the carters and departed, the girl at the table looking very small and lonely.

"Walt," the sheriff asked as they walked to the the nearby stable, "have you any notion yet of who is the head devil of the pack?"

NINE

"A notion is the right word precisely," *El Halcón* answered. "Just a vague notion, something in the nature of a hunch."

"If you've got that far, the hellion is spotted," declared Crane. "I've had my eye on a certain gent for quite a while now."

"Careful," Slade cautioned. "You could be making a bad mistake. So could I, for that matter."

"I don't buy that one little bit," the sheriff declared. "You ain't in the habit of making that kind of mistake. Well, here we are, with the boys all ready and waiting."

They cinched up quickly and set out. East by north, Slade led the way. He paid little attention to the back track, for nobody could cross the open prairie without his eyes spotting them. A little later he turned east with a southerly veering.

It was a beautiful night for a ride, so far, but in the far south was a threat of overcast later. Somewhere a dove was calling sadly, and the twinkling gleam of fireflies dusted the grasses with gold.

Mile after mile they covered, at a fairly fast pace.

After a while the sheriff remarked, "Pretty near opposite the Tumble ford."

Slade nodded and kept on riding.

"Now we are opposite it, but quite a bit to the north," Crane said. Slade nodded again, and kept on riding. The sheriff growled under his mustache, but knew better than to ask questions to which he would get no answers, *El Halcón* not being ready to talk yet. A few minutes more and Slade did speak.

"See that shadow against the northern skyline?" he asked. "That is the hills where Blake's cows are holed up right now, but they won't be much longer. Speed up a bit."

Several fast miles, and Crane observed, "We're off Kerr's holding now and on Martin Gladden's Lazy G holding."

"At the foot of which is the river and an excellent ford," Slade replied.

"So that's where they cross 'em!" snorted the sheriff.

"Exactly," Slade answered. "That's where they've always crossed, while Blake, and others, chased their tails in circles around Tumble and got exactly nowhere. Very simple."

"Uh-huh, for you," grumbled Crane. "But old cowmen are set in their ways, and when they get a notion in their blasted noodles, it takes dynamite to jerk it out. Maybe they'll do better from now on, although I doubt it. How you plan to handle things, Walt?"

"Same old procedure we have employed before," Slade replied. "Hole up in the brush close to the ford until the herd shows. The riders will shove the cows down the slope to the water and be bunched behind the herd. Then we'll hit them. We'll have to give them a chance to surrender—we're law-enforcement officers. They won't take it, so, as I've said before, shoot fast and shoot straight. It's a killer bunch and we can expect no mercy from them if they get the upper hand. Not going to be good shooting light, either. The overcast has reached us and is slowly getting heavier. Still clear to the north, however."

A little farther and Crane remarked, "Getting close to the ford."

"Yes, I can see the opening in the chaparral where the track runs down to the river."

"I can't see nothin'," grumbled the sheriff. "Those eyes of yours!"

A few hundred yards more and Slade drew rein, his eyed fixed on the north.

"Here we'll stow the horses in the brush," he said. "Then we'll ease ahead until we are close to the ford. Then wait. Nothing else to do until I spot the herd, which I figure will show very soon."

The wait proved tedious. The night was very still, with only the weird cry of some night bird to break the great hush. That and the gurgle and moan of the nearby river. Slade began to wonder uneasily if his analysis of the situation was wrong, his hunch not a straight one. Was beginning to look a little that way. The overcast was moving steadily north, but there was still enough light to distinguish large objects. At least to the eyes of *El Halcón*.

60

Finally, after what seemed an eternity of nervewracking waiting, his pulses leaped exultantly, for he saw it, quite some distance to the northwest—the moving cloud that was the marching herd. Hunch was a straight one!

"Here they come," he said. "Get ready for business."

Gradually the "shadow" discovered form and shape. A herd of more than a hundred head. A little more and the riders shoving the cows along became discernible. Slade whistled under his breath. There were seven of them! The odds were going to be uncomfortably lopsided.

But he counted heavily on the element of surprise and the fact that the posse would be on foot, the wideloopers mounted, outlined against the sky. Anyhow, they were in for it and had to make the best of what might be a bad business. However, *El Halcón* did not believe it would be. His companions were men of tried courage and excellent shots. He'd make out. He waited a few more minutes, then said, "Move down through the brush and take up position." The sheriff and the deputies followed directions.

"This should be just right. Hold it!" Slade said.

Soon the peevish bawling of the irritated cattle could be heard, growing louder and louder, then the beat of hoofs. Another short wait and down the slope barged the cows, heading for the water. And after them bunched, as Slade said they would be, the wideloopers, laughing and talking, apparently unaware of anybody within a half-score of miles. Against the dimly star-lighted sky they loomed.

"Up!" Slade thundered. "You are under arrest! In the name of the State of Texas!"

Startled exclamations, a whirling in the saddles, hands streaking to holsters.

"Let them have it!" Slade roared, and shot with both hands. The posse joined in, and the bellowing gun battle was on.

Two wideloopers fell at that first booming volley. Slade fired again, right and left. A third outlaw spun from the saddle. Answering slugs whined past, one barely grazing Slade's ribs. Behind him sounded an angry curse, and he knew somebody else was nicked. He lined sights with a rustler on a bucking, plunging horse, scored a miss. The posse shot together and a fourth outlaw was down.

A word of command was shouted. The three remaining wideloopers spun their mounts and went charging up the slope, Slade speeding them on their way with bullets. A yelp echoed the reports, but three sets of hoofs drummed east on the trail. To try to pursue the escaping trio was out of the question.

"Hold it!" he called to his companions, his gun trained on the four forms in the dust. Neither moved and he was confident there was nothing more to fear from them.

"Anybody hurt?" he asked anxiously. A burst of profanity from the sheriff answered the query as he swabbed at a slight cheek slice.

"Just a scratch," he assured the Ranger. "Scar will make me even purtier than I am now. Let's see what we bagged. Figure we didn't do too bad. Four of the devils done for and the cows saved."

By the light of matches they examined the dead outlaws. They were pronounced ornery-looking specimens. Slade reserved opinion until they could be given a more thorough examination.

The cattle had quieted and were either sucking up water or nosing at the scant grass that grew near the river's edge. The outlaw horses, well-trained beasts, had not followed the others but remained close to their fallen masters. The rigs were stripped off and they were turned loose to fend for themselves until picked up.

"Tom, you can send a wagon tomorrow to pick up the bodies," Slade said. "And you, Ester," he told the deputy, "hightail to Blake's *casa* and tell him we're shoving his cows home, and for him to meet us on the way and take care of them.

"And now, Tom," he added, "I'll put some salve and a pad on your cheek."

He whistled a loud, clear note, and in a few minutes Shadow responded, snorting disgust with everything in general. Slade secured his medicants, and despite the sheriff's protest that the scratch wasn't worth bothering with, he quickly had the wound cared for.

"That will hold you till we get to town," he said, with a final pat to the pad. "Now for the cows."

Three experienced and skillful range riders had no difficulty rounding up the thoroughly irritated critters and getting them in marching order.

But nearly four hours had passed and the riders were as disgusted as the cattle before Gird Blake and his hands hove into view to take over the chore. He was profuse in his thanks to Slade and the sheriff. Slade listened for a few minutes, then lit into him for fair.

"And if you'd pay more attention to your stock and properly patrol your holding, and give up your loco opposition to the oil field and the railroad, both of which will ultimately be to your advantage, this sort of a thing won't happen."

Blake took it meekly—he could hardly do otherwise—and promised to mend his ways.

"And that I consider something worthwhile accomplished," Slade said as they headed for Sanderson through the rosy glow of the dawn. "The chances are he'll talk with the other old coot and make him easier to line up.

"It was just a routine chore tonight. Not the first time we have frustrated a widelooping in just that way, but everything worked out very well. The great weakness of the outlaw brand is their overweening conceit, believing themselves infallible and mistakenly governing their actions accordingly. This time our bunch was convinced that everybody subscribed to the belief that the widelooped cows would cross the river by way of the Tumble ford, ignoring the chance that somebody might arrive at a different conclusion."

"Uh-huh, and ignoring *El Halcón*'s brains, and by doing so making a darn costly mistake," observed Crane. "As you say, always the little slips."

And the sheriff knew that one of the explanations of Walt Slade's uniform success against the owlhoot brand was his unique ability to put himself in their place, to think as they would think, and to recognize the little slips for what they were and govern his own actions accordingly. As Captain Jim McNelty said over and over, Walt Slade not only outshot the owlhoots, he also outthought them.

It was well past daybreak when they reached Sanderson. First they cared for their tired horses. Then they contacted old Alf, the special, and a couple of his cronies. Arrangements were made to fetch the bodies to town, and the rigs. And the outlaw horses, if they could catch them.

Next stop was the Branding Pen and something to eat. There they found Mary Merril awaiting them.

"I didn't feel like leaving until I knew you were back

safe," she told Slade. "So I sent Saxon ahead with the carts, hoping you'd ride to Echo with me tomorrow."

"The chances are I will," Slade replied. "Want another look at that pueblo; it's interesting."

After they finished eating and a smoke, Mary said, "All right, to bed with the lot of you; no doubt but that you are in need of a little sleep. Be seeing you later."

"Don't make it too long," the sheriff cautioned. "Folks get restless if kept waiting too long."

Mary ignored him.

When Slade awoke after several hours of refreshing sleep, he knew by the angle of the sun rays
seeping through the chinks in the blind that sunset was
not far off. For a while he lay conning over the recent
incidents, not without a certain satisfaction. He felt he
had made considerable headway against the owlhoot
bunch. The thwarting of the Vanstaveren store robbery
and that of the El Paso Flyer express-car robbery were
not to be lightly disregarded. Nor was the frustrating of
the attempt against Blake's cows. He believed he had given
the head of the bunch something to think about, his com-
placency a jar. A little more of the same might well bring
him out in the open. Which would be very much to his,
Slade's, advantage.

So far he had been little more than a shadow weaving
in and out among the shadows. And had he not made
the very small slip that convinced *El Halcón* he was other
than what he seemed and pretended to be, he might still
be safe in the shadows. As it was, Slade was confident
it was but a matter of time until he was unmasked and
revealed for what he was.

That unmasking him would not be a simple matter,
Slade readily conceded. He was shrewd, with a quick
mind, and utterly ruthless. Well, he had gone up against
that sort before and had always made out. No reason
why this should prove the exception to the rule.

Anyhow, there should be a peaceful day or two. The
hellion would hardly pull something in a hurry after
the debacle of the night before.

Which went to show that even *El Halcón* could guess
wrong now and then.

He arose, cleaned up a bit, dressed, and made his
way to the Branding Pen, where he found the sheriff
comfortable with a snort and his pipe.

A few minutes later Mary joined them. The sheriff
twinkled his eyes. Mary wrinkled her pert nose at him.

"I'm hungry," she said. Slade beckoned a waiter.

"Walt, do you figure one of the three devils who got

65

in the clear last night was the he-wolf of the pack?" the sheriff asked.

"Yes, I think the one who ordered the other two to sift sand is the head man," Slade replied. "The way he sized up the situation and reacted evinced fast thinking, as would be expected from the leader."

"Sort of on the big side, wasn't he?" Crane observed. "Not too tall, but plenty big."

"So it seemed to me," Slade answered. "However, I didn't get anything like a good look at him. He was into the brush almost as quickly as he shouted."

"Hmmm!" remarked the sheriff. Slade shot him a warning glance. Mary's graceful black brows drew together slightly, but she did not comment.

Food arrived shortly, and for a while conversation languished.

"Another snort to hold the chuck down and I'm rarin' to go," said the sheriff. "Not that I got any notion where I'm going, but I'm on the way."

Mary glanced out the window and sprang to her feet. "Come on, Walt," she said. "I want to watch the sunset."

Slade agreed. The sheriff ordered another snort and announced his intention of staying right where he was. Slade and Mary left the Branding Pen together, walking slowly along the bustling streets until they reached the south edge of town. There they stood gazing at the stupendous fantasy of beauty spread before their eyes.

The mountains stood in somber grandeur, their towering crests bursts of flame. The sky was already a riot of color, from the blazing scarlet of the west to the soft rose of the east. Crimson and gold and pulsing vermilion vied one with the other to dominate the scene, while on the far horizon was the first faint shadow of the conquering night.

In silence they watched until the vivid hues faded and in the steel-blue vault of the heavens a great star glowed and trembled.

Still silent, they walked back to the Branding Pen. The sheriff glanced up expectantly.

"Nice walk?" he asked.

"Very," Mary replied. "The sunset was beautiful, and there is one thing particularly nice about Walt."

"Guess you should know," the sheriff agreed cheerfully.

"Yes," said Mary. "A characteristic others I might mention would do well to emulate. He knows when not to talk!"

The sheriff looked as if he could comment on that one, but refrained from doing so.

"I want a glass of wine and then I want to dance," Mary said. Both lacks were cared for.

The hours jogged along, gay, turbulent, but with everybody apparently on good behavior. Sanderson was having a comparatively peaceful night.

It was different elsewhere. Tumble, the oil town to the southeast, was booming per usual. The streets were crowded and bustling with a jostling, whooping throng. Song, or what was apparently intended for it, poured over the swinging doors, with a constant patter of whirling words. The click of high heels and the thump of boots sounded from the dance floors. The chink of bottlenecks on glass rims and the clang of gold pieces on the mahogany provided a sprightly accompaniment to the general hullabaloo.

The bars were packed with oil workers, railroad builders, and cowhands, all raising old Harry to the best of their ability. To paraphrase that old western doggerel, Tumble was

> Wild and wooly and full of fleas,
> Hard to curry below the knees!

Hardrock Hogan's Branding Pen Two was doing plenty of business. The same went for the Good Enough Saloon at the edge of the oil field. It was nearly as big as the Branding Pen but not so well furnished. It catered to the younger and rowdier elements.

For quite a while the owners of the various establishments had heeded Walt Slade's warning against keeping large sums of money on their premises, a temptation to the outlaw fraternity. But of late, with nothing untoward happening, they had grown careless.

So Paul Menard, the comparatively new owner of the Good Enough, sat in his back room with the back door locked and tallied nearly two weeks' take, packets of big bills, rolls of gold coins.

From the saloon came the usual racket, muffled by the closed door, but Menard, absorbed in his figuring, paid little attention to it. His bartenders and floor men were dependable and kept their eyes open and an especial watch on that door to the back room.

From a stand of thicket back of the building that housed the Good Enough Saloon shot something that trailed sparks through the air. It was an arrow wrapped with oil-soaked cotton waste. It struck the tinder-dry shingles of the Good Enough building roof and instantly burst into flame, the fire licking the shingles, which immediately blazed up. A few minutes passed, then resounded that most terrible cry in the night:

"Fire!"

The Good Enough patrons looked up from their drinks, saw smoke pouring down the stairs from the second floor, heard the wild shouting outside. They emptied the saloon, along with the help, in little more than a matter of seconds.

All except three men who lingered behind in the smoke, jerking their hatbrims down low, jerking their neckerchiefs up high, so that little more than their eyes was discernible.

In the back room, Menard, the owner, was raking his money on the table together when the door from the smoke-filled saloon crashed open and the three masked men barged in.

Menard made a grab for the old Smith & Wesson in the table drawer, but too late. A gun barrel crashed against his skull and stretched him dazed and bleeding and helpless on the floor. The robbers scooped up the money, dropped it into a sack one carried, and groped their way through the smoke and sparks to the outside, leaving Menard to the mercy of the flames. They mingled with the crowd, and a few moments later fast hoofs drummed from the thicket, eastward.

It was the head bartender who proved to be the hero of the occasion.

"My God!" he suddenly exclaimed. "Where's the boss? He must still be in the back room!"

Ducking his head and shielding his face with his arm, he

68

dashed back into the burning building, managed to make it to the back room, seized the helpless owner by the collar and, gasping and choking, dragged him to the outside, where he collapsed beside him. Ready hands moved both away from the building and ministered to them.

A bucket brigade had quickly been formed, and the workers, trained to cope with emergencies, finally got the fire under control. Only the roof and part of the second story suffered damage.

Menard had recovered full consciousness and reported his loss.

"But to hell with it," he said. "It was only money. Just so nobody, including myself, got burned up. Send word to Sheriff Crane at Sanderson; he'll want to know about it, although I can't see there's anything he can do. The devils are gone."

"And fetch Doc Cooper," somebody added. "He'll want to take a look at Menard's head."

An oldtimer experienced in such matters insisted on giving the scalp cut a once-over despite Menard's protests that it wasn't worth bothering with. After an examination he rendered the opinion that the wound was not serious. He applied salve and a pad, and opined, "Guess that'll hold you till Doc gets here."

"And now everybody come in and have one on the house," Menard said, an invitation such a gathering was loath to refuse. And after the free drink, they lingered to buy.

"At this rate I'll break even before the night's over," Menard chuckled to his head bartender. "And believe me, *you* are in for a nice fat bonus."

"Wasn't anything to it," replied the barkeep. "Just like draggin' a drunk out—good practice. Thank Pete it ain't raining, and hope it won't until we get that roof patched."

The messenger who, knowing there was no hurry, had lingered to partake of Menard's hospitality, reached Sanderson shortly before midmorning and quickly contacted the early-rising sheriff.

"I'll ride down there this afternoon," Crane said after listening to the account of the depredation. "Go over to the Branding Pen and have a drink on me, a couple of 'em. I'll have a deputy get in touch with Doc Cooper."

Crane saw no sense in rousing up Slade and waited until the Ranger put in an appearance about an hour later.

"Yes, we'll ride down," *El Halcón* said. "Might be able to hit on something of interest. Looks like folks will never learn. If Menard had done what he was supposed to do instead of letting his money pile up, it wouldn't have happened. Well, let's go eat; Mary will meet us at the Branding Pen."

In the Branding Pen, Mary immediately announced her purpose to ride with them to Tumble.

"I want to contact some of the folks there," she said. "If they are in need of something, I'll divert the carts from Echo to a run to Tumble."

"A good idea," Slade agreed. "Especially if you decide to obtain more carts, the notion I know you're toying with."

"And if I go along, maybe I can keep you out of trouble for another night," she said.

"Maybe," said the sheriff. "There's trouble and trouble."

Mary ignored him.

As they headed for Tumble, the sheriff suddenly remarked, "Well, looks like we'll have to chalk one up for his side. He made a good haul."

"Definitely," Slade conceded. "And I was neatly outsmarted with my erroneous opinion that he wouldn't attempt anything right after what happened to his widelooping try."

"Don't see how you could have figured anything else," was Crane's consoling reply. "How could anybody figure in advance just what he would do, with so many things he could do. A sorta original caper, emptying the saloon by setting the roof on fire."

"Yes, nothing will clear folks out of a place faster than the realization the building is on fire over their heads. Very clever."

"According to the messenger, Menard took it in stride," the sheriff observed. "Said it was only money and nobody was bad hurt."

"Evidently a very remarkable fellow," Slade said. "Undoubtedly a philosopher."

"Ain't nothing to look at," replied the sheriff. "Scrawny little coot. Guess that was in his favor, though. If he'd been big and husky, the chances are the bartender wouldn't have been able to haul him out before he suffocated. Wonder how the devil they managed to set the house afire?"

"I'd say the explanation is very simple," Slade answered. "Took a page from the oldtime Indians' book, who used to shoot flaming arrows onto the covered wagons and set them afire over the heads of the defenders. I'll look things over when we get there."

"If you say that's the way it was done, guess it was," said the sheriff. "Well, anyhow it's a nice day for a ride. How you making out, Mary?"

"Quietly enjoying myself," the girl replied.

"She too knows when not to talk," Slade said. "Not that she's had much chance, with us jabbering away like we have been."

"I gathered Menard wasn't much hurt," the sheriff observed. "But to make sure, Doc Cooper rode down with Deputy Ester."

"The wise thing to do," Slade returned. "Best not to take chances with a head wound."

A few miles farther and they sighted the smoke smudge that hovered over the oil field, and half an hour later they reached Tumble.

They stabled their horses and repaired to Branding Pen Two, where they found Deputy Ester and the doctor putting away a snack.

"Menard is all right," Cooper said. "No indications of fracture or concussion; he'll make out."

Mary decided to remain in the saloon while Slade and Crane visited the Good Enough, there being some oilmen present she wished to talk with.

Menard, a spry little man with bright eyes and a crackling voice, greeted them warmly but could tell them little they didn't already know. No, he didn't get a good look at the devils who struck him down, wouldn't recognize them did he see them again. The bartender vaguely recalled three men standing near the end of the bar but had paid them no mind, strangers being too common to the Good Enough to attract any attention.

Slade investigated the thicket back of the building. "Four horses were tethered here," he announced. "Evidently the one who shot the burning arrow onto the roof remained in the thicket until the others showed with the money. Nothing we can do, so far as I can see. The hellion put one over and that's all there is to it."

Crane gazed up at the carpenters working on the roof, filling the air with the click of hammers and the rasping of saws.

"Guess they'll have the repairs finished by this time tomorrow," he said. "Well, how about back to Branding Pen Two and a snort and something to eat? Soon be dark."

"A notion," Slade agreed. "Sure for certain Mary is hungry by now, and I feel I could stand a small helping myself."

Through the deepening dusk they walked back to the saloon, where Mary was talking with several oilmen. However, she quickly terminated the conversation and trotted to the table.

"Well, I let myself in for it," she announced. "I'll have a cart train rolling this way in a couple of days. No rest for the wicked, and darn little for the righteous. Guess I have no right to complain, seeing as you two managed to get back to me without getting mixed up in some sort of a ruckus. I'm hungry!"

"Makes two of us, maybe three," said the sheriff. "Hey! look at who's down at the end of the bar."

Slade had already noticed the big man talking with the head bartender. It was Vince Rader, owner of the Diehard saloon in Echo.

"Gent gets around," he remarked.

"He sure does," growled the sheriff, his brows drawing together as he regarded the saloonkeeper. "Funny how he shows up so pat—at certain times."

Slade shook his head and the sheriff subdued to grunts and mutters.

"Deputy Ester and the doctor dropped over to the office to see if everything is okay there," Mary remarked. "Said they'd be back soon."

"We won't wait on 'em," said Crane. "Waiter!"

The waiter responded, and soon the companions had a tasty meal set before them.

When they finished eating, Slade went back to the kitchen to thank the cook and have a word with him and his assistants, lithe young Yaqui-Mexicans.

"I may need your help again soon," he told them.

"To assist *El Halcón* is the honor great," they replied, bowing low. "When *Capitán* calls, we are ready."

Slade knew they would be as good as their word. After a final good night, he returned to his table.

Vince Rader strolled over from the end of the bar.

"Sit down and have a drink," Slade invited.

"Don't mind if I do," Rader accepted. "How are you, Mr. Slade? And you, Sheriff? And you, Miss Merril? You've sure got a lot of friends here, Miss Merril. They are singing your praises down at the end of the bar."

"It isn't me with whom they are enamored," Mary smiled. "It's the loads of casings and other materials I bring them."

"Oh, those are just incidentals," Rader differed. "By the way, understand they had quite a bit of excitement here last night."

"So we gather," Slade replied. "That's why we happened to ride down here instead of to Echo as originally planned."

"I was down at the Good Enough this afternoon," Rader said. "Had a talk with Menard. Glad nothing bad happened to him. 'Pears to be a nice little fellow."

"Struck me that way," Slade conceded. "He got a lucky break in his bartender being so on the alert. Otherwise he might well have suffocated in that back room. You interested in Tumble, Mr. Rader?"

"Not particularly, at least so far," Rader answered. "I

had planned to ride to Sanderson for a gabfest with my old *amigo* Hardrock Hogan, and then decided while I was at it to go by way of Tumble, look the town over, and then head for Sanderson tomorrow.

"I suppose, Mr. Slade, that Hardrock told you that quite some years back we were prospectors together. Then after a bit we separated and lost track of each other. Hardrock stayed in Texas; I went to California, where I too made a lucky strike, not as big a one as Hardrock made, but plenty big enough to set me up in a business I figured would pay off, the saloon business." He sipped his drink, and chuckled.

"Mr. Slade," he resumed, "chuck-line-riding cowhands, wildcat oil drillers, and prospectors are in the same category, always on the lookout for something new. Right now Hardrock, although he already owns two prosperous businesses, is toying with the notion of setting up a third in Echo. And I'll have to admit that I came to Tumble with something of the same idea in my mind."

Meanwhile, Mary and the sheriff had sat silent, for both knew what Rader didn't know, that *El Halcón* was inducing the saloon owner to talk about himself, carefully checking what he said against what he, Slade, already knew concerning him.

Rader insisted on buying a round of drinks. After he emptied his glass, he stood up, smiling.

"Going to prowl around a bit and look things over," he said. "May see you all a little later, can't tell."

Slade also stood up, and shook hands with Rader, who looked pleased. He waved to the others and departed.

Mary and the sheriff had been watching Slade closely; now the latter said, with a sigh, "So out the window that one goes, right?"

Slade nodded, smilingly. "Not that I ever considered him very seriously as a suspect. He just didn't fit into the picture properly. The big wooly bear type, as Mary would say, and big wooly bears aren't subtle or devious; they charge direct or not at all."

"And who does that leave?" snorted Crane.

"The real head of the bunch," Slade answered, still smiling, but with a grim look in the depths of his eyes. "I'm not quite ready to name names, but I expect to be soon."

His hearers did not press for added information, knowing it would be just a waste of time to do so.

Deputy Ester and Doc Cooper strolled in and drew up chairs.

"Was beginning to think you'd got lost in the shuffle," Crane observed.

"Caught up with some paperwork and then sat and smoked and talked for a while," the deputy explained. Slade summoned a waiter.

"I think you'd better stick around here for a few days and keep an eye on things," the sheriff said to the deputy.

"A good notion," agreed Ester.

The night wore on, noisy and boisterous, as Tumble always was, but with no untoward incident. Finally Mary glanced at the clock, stifled a yawn with a pink palm, and said, "I'm going upstairs to bed. It's been a long and hard day."

"And shortly I'll emulate your example," Slade replied. He opened the stair door for her and held it open until she reached the second floor where she always had a room reserved.

Crane decided on a last snort of redeye, and then he and Ester and the doctor headed for his office, there being bunks in the back room for their accommodation. Slade went upstairs to his room.

Slade was astir early, for he wished to have a few words with Broderick, the railroad construction engineer, before riding to Echo. He decided to forego breakfast for the time being, and after a cup of coffee he rode slowly north along the twin steel ribbons, carefully scanning the construction.

The ties were properly spaced; there was plenty of clearance between the butt ends of the rails to care for expansion and contraction of the steel due to weather changes. Broderick was a good engineer and knew his business.

About three miles farther on was the railhead, a scene of bustling activity. A big locomotive shoved a long string of cars loaded with rails, ties, fish plates, and other materials which the busy workers were dumping. Everywhere was orderly confusion.

Broderick greeted Slade with enthusiasm. "Well, think

Mr. Dunn will be satisfied with the progress being made?" he asked.

"He certainly will," Slade replied; "you're doing fine. Any trouble?"

"Nope," Broderick said. "Now and then there are horsemen who 'pear to be keeping tabs on what's going on, but they have never ridden close. Just idle curiosity, I imagine."

Slade was scanning the terrain. Nearly a thousand yards to the east was a low brush-covered hill with a flat crest. He studied it with care.

"There's somebody on that hilltop right now," he remarked.

"I can't see anything," Broderick replied.

"He's there, all right," Slade said, dropping a hand to his high-power Winchester snugged in the saddle boot.

From the edge of the hill crest gushed a puff of smoke, followed by the clang of a shot. A slug whined past, high overhead. Broderick uttered a startled exclamation. The workers ceased their activities to stare at the hilltop.

"So! Want to play games, eh?" Slade said. He whipped out the Winchester and sprayed the hill crest with bullets, purposely holding high, for he had no desire to kill somebody were it not necessary.

The tops of the chaparral growth were violently agitated as if something was dashing through it, very likely a horse. Slade laughed.

"What does it mean?" wondered Broderick.

"Hellion wasn't trying to score a hit, not at that distance," *El Halcón* answered. "Just aimed to startle the men and slow up the work."

"Hey!" shouted Broderick. "Here comes a bunch of the devils!"

Swerving around the hill to the north were half a score of riders. There followed a crackle of shots.

"What in the world!" exclaimed the engineer. Slade laughed again.

"I'd say," he replied, "that old Gird Blake's boys don't intend to stand for any nonsense when the steel begins crossing his holding. Those riders were also keeping tabs on things, for a different reason."

He recounted, briefly, the thwarted attempt to wideloop Blake's cattle, for which the owner was profoundly grateful and evidently determined to express his gratitude in a practical manner.

"So," Slade concluded, "I don't think you need fear any serious trouble before the last five or six miles, and perhaps before then I will manage to show that other old coot of an owner the error of his ways."

"I don't know what we would do without you," Broderick sighed.

"Okay, fellows," he called to the workers. "Mr. Slade says everything is under control and nothing to bother about."

"If he say so, guess it is," came the reply. Wrenches began screaking again, hammers thudding.

Blake's riders reappeared, heading north at a fast pace. Broderick watched them.

"Wonder if they caught up with the devil?" he remarked.

"I'd say no," Slade answered. "He had a start, and besides I doubt they really desired to catch up with him. Satisfied just to give him a good scare. Well, I'm returning to Tumble and some breakfast. Keep the good work going. I'll be seeing you again before long." He turned Shadow and rode swiftly back to town.

When he entered Branding Pen Two, Mary and the sheriff were awaiting him.

"Now what?" the girl asked accusingly.

"Just took a little ride to work up an appetite," the Ranger replied. Mary sniffed daintily.

"A likely story," she said.

"Anyhow, I didn't get any decorations for Tom's office floor," he pointed out. "Which certainly indicates good behavior on my part."

"Time that grinds the rocks will tell us all," Mary quoted. "I'm hungry."

After they had finished a leisurely breakfast, she said, "And now I'm all set for Echo. You riding with us, Uncle Tom?"

"Guess I will," the sheriff decided. "Doc Cooper headed for Sanderson and Deputy Ester will keep an eye on things here. Perhaps there'll be something interesting in Echo."

"I can do without it, whatever it is," Mary declared. "Your and Walt's notion of something interesting usually gives me the creeps."

It was a beautiful day for a ride. Roses were blooming, the thorn briars in fruit. In the west a towering thunderhead pulsed and palpitated, throwing back the sunlight in shimmering waves that discounted its potential of crashing storm.

Birds sang in the thickets. Little animals darted to and fro. Sunshine and peace!

But even as the threat of the thunderhead, the shadow of evil hovered over the quiet rangeland.

Without misadventure they reached Echo as the sunset blazed its glory, to find the town wild with excitement. One of the drills had brought in Echo's first gusher!

Men were working madly to cap the well and bring it under control by a firmly anchored valve, while they lustily caroled a rousing old song of the gold-rush times:

> "The days of old!
> The days of gold!
> The days of Forty-nine!"

"And Forty-nine was picayune to what Echo is going to be," was declared on all sides.

Slade and his companions rode through the **TWELVE** excitement without drawing rein until they reached Lerner's place. They stabled their horses and sat down with wine, coffee, and a snort to await the arrival of the magnate, who was supervising the capping of the well.

He arrived shortly, his eyes snapping. "The answer to the doubting Thomases who said we'd never strike a pool here," he chuckled, jerking his thumb toward the field. "Guess they'll sing another song now."

Farsighted, he already had tanks building to store the flow.

"And I'm sending word to the railroaders to stir their stumps and get us tank cars here for shipment."

"I'll arrange to have a night crew on the job," Slade said.

"That'll be fine!" enthused Lerner. He repeated Broderick's words: "I don't know what we'd do without you."

"You'd make out," Slade predicted cheerfully. "You did for quite a while before you and I got together."

"What do you think about it, Mary?" Lerner asked.

"Sometimes I think he's the reward for good living, at others that he's a curse sent upon me for my sins," the blue-eyed girl replied. Lerner and the sheriff shook with laughter.

"I'll tell the cook to get busy," the former said. "All this excitement makes me hungry."

"Me, too," chimed in Mary.

Slade and the sheriff evinced a willingness to take a chance, and shortly they drew up their chairs to an appetizing repast, to which they all did full justice.

After they finished their meal, Mary sipped her wine while the men smoked and talked. When her glass was empty, she said, "And now I want to do the town. Sure sounds interesting tonight."

"Too darn interesting," growled the sheriff. "If something off-color don't come of it I miss my guess."

"Uncle Tom, you're a hypocritical pessimist," Mary

79

told him. "You love it just like the rest of us but won't admit it."

The sheriff snorted but declined to get into an argument. "Let's go," he said.

"How about the Wallop first?" Slade suggested. Nobody objected.

When they entered, they found the place quite different from the time of their former visit. There were now plenty of tables, the lunch counter was functioning, the kitchen going full blast. The rooms to which the doors led were evidently completed. The back bar boasted a wide mirror.

Slade thought there was an amused gleam in Norton's pale eyes when he greeted them.

"Keeps me scratching to meet the bills, but I believe it will pay off in the end," he said in his high, musical voice when complimented on the improvements.

"No doubt as to that," the sheriff agreed. Slade nodded.

After what happened later that night, Slade half wondered could the threatening thunderhead have been an omen, although he never put much faith in omens.

They had a couple of drinks with Norton, then sallied forth onto the roaring streets.

"Even worse than a payday," Crane declared as they shoved their way through the jostling, bellowing crowds, each street as they drew near the field seeming worse than the preceding one.

After a hard fight of it, they finally reached the Diehard and dived in to catch their breath, although it wasn't much better than the outside.

Anyhow, there was a table and chairs, to which Rader's headwaiter conducted them, which enabled them to give their feet a rest.

"Mine have been stepped on until they are sore," Mary said. "Just the same, though, I think it's all wonderful. I'm having a really good time."

"No accounting for tastes," growled the sheriff, sampling his drink.

"As I said before, feller knows his whiskey," he added. "Have to give him credit for that. Looks like nearly all your carters are at the bar, Mary. They've sure taken to the darn rumhole."

"Let them have their fun," the girl replied. "Tomorrow they'll roll the empties to Sanderson, and by that time I'll have made up my mind just what to do. I'm likely to send a train to Tumble next, with materials they are badly in need of there, if I decide Echo can wait for a couple of days. Oh, well, forget business for the time being. I want to just relax and enjoy myself while I have the chance."

The hours glided past, the clock hands approaching midnight, with no lessening of the Echo oil-strike celebration. Hard to tell which was the noisiest, the streets or the saloons. The din in the Diehard was deafening, the air thick with tobacco smoke. But nobody seemed to mind.

Slade, however, was growing just a little weary of the smoke and the racket, and was hoping for an opportunity to escape it for a while.

The opportunity was provided. Lerner asked Mary to dance, and they moved onto the crowded floor. The sheriff was at the bar talking with some acquaintances. Slade got to his feet, glanced around, and without attracting any attention, slipped through the swinging doors and onto the jam-packed street, where at least there was less smoke, and more space for the noise to dissipate.

For a while he wandered about aimlessly. Finally, however, he made his way south to where the trail slithered down the slope. Now he was beyond the area of saloons and other attractions and there was nobody near and the noise was but a rumble and mutter. He rolled a cigarette, leaned against a convenient tree trunk and stood gazing up the trail to the bristling crest outlined against the starry sky.

Quiet and peaceful, but a deceptive peace. Abruptly he straightened, staring.

At the lip of the brush-grown crest was a flicker, a glow, a burst of flame. And at the same instant he heard a drumming of fast hoofs down the trail.

From the mouth of the trail bulged two horsemen. They spotted *El Halcón* at once. Startled exclamations, and both streaked hands to their holsters.

Slade drew and shot, left and right. Answering slugs fanned his face as he dodged and ducked. One turned his hat sideways on his head. Another just grazed his forehead, throwing him off balance for a moment.

But already one of the gun slingers was down, sprawled in the dust. His companion took deliberate aim and squeezed trigger.

But just a split second too late. He fell, his breast riddled and smashed by the Ranger's bullets, to also lie without sound or motion.

Roaring and popping and crackling, the crest was a tossing, blinding tempest of flame that was seething down the slope. With scarce a glance at the two dead outlaws, Slade rushed back to the town, roaring "Fire!" at the top of his voice.

"Water!" he thundered. "Get buckets and water! Drench the roofs. Another minute and sparks and brands will be falling on them! The whole town will go up in smoke! Move! Start down this way and work north!"

Now the saloons were emptying. Men in the street were already doing as Slade ordered. And these were men for whom such an emergency held no real terrors. It was just a chore that had to be done. Without an instant's delay they did battle with the fire demon.

Most fortunately, there was plenty of water available, there being a number of big springs in the basin. And thanks to the carpenters, there were numbers of ladders to be had. Soon water was streaming from the roofs. Flickers were stamped out.

But for a while it was touch and go. On three sides of the basin was a veritable holocaust of flame and billowing smoke. Only to the north was the air comparatively clear.

Slade was everywhere, directing, encouraging, using his great strength to the best advantage. Beside him were Mary Merril, a scarf tied over her hair, and Westbrook Lerner. All three were blackened by smoke, streaked with ashes, but they never faltered.

"Your carts and mules are safe," Slade told the girl. "The boys saw to that first off."

"To heck with the carts," she replied. "But I'm glad the poor mules are all right. This is terrible, but with a wonderful, wild beauty. The tops of the growth burst like skyrockets. And look at those crimson spirals, flowing off on all sides like red lava streams. The firmament above is a reflected hell, but gorgeous. I suppose I'm awful, but I can't help but love it!"

"A girl to ride the river with," Lerner murmured. Slade nodded emphatically.

The heat in the basin was terrific, but the strong up-draft took care of the worst of the smoke, which helped.

Gradually the battle was won. The fire was dying down for lack of anything more to consume. A little more water on the buildings closest to the slopes, the derricks inspected, with careful attention given to the sheds that housed the machinery.

"Everything pretty well under control," Slade said.

"Thank Heaven we got that well capped before it happened," remarked Lerner. Had the oil been still flowing we would have had something it is doubtful we would have been able to control. And the same goes for you catching on and getting the work started so fast. How in the world did it happen to catch, do you know?"

"Come along and I'll show you," Slade replied. "We'll stop at the Diehard and pick up the sheriff."

As Slade expected, they found the smoke-blackened sheriff at the Diehard.

"All right," he said, "where are the carcasses? The shooting was heard, but before we could investigate that, all hell cut loose. What took place?"

Slade told him, briefly, of his brush with the firebugs. The sheriff did some fancy swearing under his mustache.

"And if you hadn't been on the job they would have gotten in the clear," he concluded.

"It is possible," Slade conceded.

As they headed for the mouth of the trail where there were still a few smolders, most of the carters and other Diehard patrons streamed after them.

"There they are," Slade said. "They fell this side of the fire. Over there are their horses. Somebody lead them to Mr. Lerner's stable and remove the rigs."

With the others watching, he and the sheriff gave the slain outlaws a brief once-over, Slade paying particular attention to their hands, and pointing out that although both had once been cowhands, they hadn't followed a cow's tail for a very long time.

"Evidence that they were not working hands for any of the spreads hereabouts," said the sheriff. Which statement was received with sober nods.

And came the inevitable question: "If it ain't the cattlemen making the trouble, who is it?"

"Which matter I hope to take care of," Slade replied. More nods.

Ornery-looking hellions, and got just what was coming to them was the consensus of opinion. Slade thought they were about average so far as appearances went, but was willing to concede that the ruthless devils got what was coming to them. Had the fire really gotten out of hand there might easily have been a loss of life.

"I'll send them to Sanderson in a cart," Lerner volunteered.

"That'll help," said Crane. "And now—"

"And now I'm for my room and a good wash and cleanup in general," Mary broke in. "I feel and look like an escapee from a smokehouse."

"A pretty good imitation of a smokehouse, a little while ago," said the sheriff. "A pity we didn't have some hams to hang up."

"Fire never got as far as my place," Lerner remarked. "Nothing up this way for it to burn."

"Nor to the Wallop saloon," Slade observed.

"That's right," agreed Lerner. "Norton's place was safe, too. Clean in there, so suppose we drop in for a last drink after a bit."

When they entered the Wallop, Slade noted that while there was still a gleam in Frederick Norton's eyes, it was no longer a gleam of amusement; it had been replaced by a gleam of anger and bafflement. He smiled slightly to himself as he sipped his coffee.

After coffee and drinks were finished, everybody agreed to call it a night.

The following afternoon the empty carts **THIRTEEN**
rolled out of smoke-smudged Echo,
bound for Sanderson. Slade and the sheriff rode with them.

"One load to Tumble and then back to Echo, if it's
okay with you," Mary said to Lerner.

"Go to it," the magnate replied. "We've got enough
casings and other materials to hold us for a few days, what
with the cleaning up and so forth we have to do."

As soon as they reached Sanderson, Slade at once sent
an urgent telegram to General Manager Dunn of the C. &
P. Railroad system. With the result that three days later a
night shift was on the job, shoving the railroad to Echo at
top speed and without hindrance of any sort, for now
the steel was passing over Gird Blake's land and old Gird's
riders were keeping an eye on things.

Meanwhile Mary had rolled a train of materials to Tumble and her empties were back in Sanderson and loading
for Echo.

"And I hope you and Uncle Tom will ride with us," she
said to Slade.

"I think we will," *El Halcón* replied. "Sanderson is
peaceful as an old maids' picnic, at least for the present.
I've a feeling conditions may be different at Echo. Anyhow I think it might be a good notion to try and find out."

That evening Slade and the sheriff sat in the office and
talked over cups of steaming coffee and smokes. Crane
was silent for some time, then he abruptly asked a question.

"Well," he said, "aren't you about ready to name a few
names—one, anyway?"

"Yes, I think I am," the Ranger replied. "Now that I
have arrived at a definite conclusion relative to the hellion,
it's best for you to know, especially as we're going to
Echo. The head man of the outlaw bunch is—Fred Norton, the Wallop owner."

The sheriff blinked and stared. "Norton!" he repeated.
"Why I never gave him a thought."

"You were concentrating too heavily on Vince Rader of

the Diehard," Slade smiled. "For a while you couldn't think of anybody else."

"Guess that's so," Crane conceded. "How'd you come to get a line on the hellion?"

"First, because he consistently lied about something," Slade replied.

"Lied about something?"

"That's right. You'll recall how he constantly harps on how he has to scratch to get money enough to meet the bills for the improvements of his place. But I learned that he has a very large sum deposited to his credit at the Sanderson Bank, money sent from a Laredo bank. Prima facie evidence he was something different from what he set up to be, a hard-working saloonkeeper trying to make a go of it. Which naturally interested me in the gentleman. And making me wonder a little about the frequent rides he took that came so pat with something off-color taking place."

"I can see that," interjected the sheriff. "Beginning to look like you're making a case against the sidewinder. What else?"

"His voice."

"His voice?"

"That's right. Norton has a high-pitched, musical voice. I never forget voices any more than I forget faces. Twice I heard the head of the pack call orders to his men, and each time he spoke in the high-pitched, musical voice I had already associated with Norton. I was confident Norton was my man. Always the little slips. Always they make them."

"Uh-huh, for somebody like you who can recognize 'em," said the sheriff. "Anything else?"

"Setting the brush fire that might have destroyed half of Echo clenched the case against him so far as I was concerned," Slade answered.

"Why the devil did he do that?" Crane wondered.

"Two reasons, I'd say," *El Halcón* replied. "Had it worked out as he planned, it would have destroyed or delayed a good deal of competition and made his place more prosperous. And it might well have heightened the friction between the field and the railroad and the cattlemen. We still have Nate Chambrun and his Forked N to deal with, and he's a cantankerous old cuss, living in the past and with no use for progress of any kind.

"And Mr. Dunn is anxious to not have to invoke Eminent Domain to drive the steel across his holding. He'd much rather make an amicable arrangement with Chambrun."

"I see," nodded the sheriff. "Going to tell Mary and Lerner what you told me?"

"Lerner, later," Slade said. "Mary has already guessed. She always gets the jump on everybody, and she reads me like a book. She knows what I'm thinking before I'm really thinking it. Which sounds rather ambiguous, but isn't where she is concerned."

"Oh, she's some gal," Crane chuckled. "They don't come any better, or any smarter. Well, what are we going to do about that horned toad now you've got him spotted?"

"Watch and wait until he tips his hand," Slade answered.

"Or until you tip it for him, which I predict will eventually be what happens," Crane said.

"Your confidence is inspiring," Slade smiled. "I hope it won't be misplaced."

"It won't be," grunted the sheriff. "Be just the same as it's always been in the past. Just a matter of time. And speaking of time and the way it passes, I figure we'd better amble over to the Branding Pen and tie onto a bite to eat."

"Best thing you've said yet," Slade replied. "Let's go!"

When they arrived at the Branding Pen, they found Mary awaiting them. Keeping her company was Vince Rader, the Diehard owner. He shook hands with Slade with great warmth.

"Just had to ride down and thank you for saving my property, Mr. Slade," he said. "It would have been a disastrous loss; no insurance yet, you know. The whole town owes you a vote of thanks."

"Now never mind a display of false modesty," Mary interjected as Slade started to speak. "You know as do the rest of us that you saved the town from going up in smoke, even if you won't admit it."

"I got the breaks," Slade protested.

"Yes," smiled Rader, "like outshooting a couple of tough gunmen. Some break!"

"They were caught by surprise," Slade replied. "And it

was a pure fluke of chance that I happened to be where I was at the time. I'd merely gone out for a while to escape the din and the smoke. Just happened to turn my steps in the direction of the trail down the slope."

His hearers did not appear impressed. He deftly got them on another subject for the moment by announcing he was hungry, and beckoned a waiter. Which guaranteed a minimum of conversation for a while.

And after they had finished eating, the carters, their chore of loading completed, roared in to provide diversions of various sorts.

"Say!" the sheriff suddenly exclaimed when he and Slade were alone for a few minutes, Mary and Rader being on dance floor. "Was that money in the Flyer express car you kept from being robbed Norton's dinero sent to his account from Laredo?"

"It was," Slade replied, smiling, for he knew what was coming.

"But heck!" Crane said. "Why should he be robbing himself?"

"He would not have been robbing himself," Slade explained. "He would have been robbing the express company, which would have had to make good the loss. Besides, there was a lot more money in that car, consigned to Marathon and El Paso. That would have been divided among him and his men, making a very nice haul in addition to the express-company insurance money."

"The ornery wind spider!" the sheriff exploded.

"Oh, he's a clever one, all right," Slade said. "Can't say as I ever went up against a smarter."

"Uh-huh, but he is going up against somebody a darn sight smarter," declared Crane. "Which he's due to find out."

Slade laughed and did not argue the point.

He had a few dances with Mary while Rader talked with Hardrock Hogan and the sheriff enjoyed his snorts and his pipe. But it had been a long and hard day, with a similar one just around the corner of the clock, so everybody called it an early night.

The carts rolled the following morning. Slade, Rader, and the sheriff rode with them.

"And with my eye on all three of you, perhaps I'll be

able to keep you out of trouble," Mary said. "I greatly fear Mr. Rader is as bad as you two. Uncle Hardrock has been telling me things about him."

Rader looked decidedly disconcerted. "Hardrock's a great liar," he muttered.

"Yes?" Mary retorted. "I've always found him painfully truthful."

Slade and the sheriff chuckled. Rader grinned sheepishly. Shadow's snort was derisive.

Today there was no ominous thunderhead towering in the west. Slade chided himself for harboring such a thought, but was forced to admit that he felt a trifle relieved.

But coming events do not necessarily cast their shadow in advance. Sometimes just the opposite.

They found Echo still somewhat smudged, but with the work of cleaning up going on apace. Another gusher had come in, and Lerner had ordered all drilling stopped until more storage tanks were completed to care for the flow.

"And we can sure use those tank cars," he said to Slade.

"You'll get them," *El Halcón* promised. "The railroad boys are sifting sand."

"What about Chambrun and his holding?" the oilman asked.

"He is still my problem," Slade replied. "The steel is very close to his land now. Well, we'll see. Perhaps our old *amigo* Fate will condescend to lend us a hand."

Which was exactly what Fate would do.

It still lacked quite a while till dark, so the unloading began without delay, the recipients of the loads gladly lending a hand.

With Lerner supervising the unloading, Mary retired to her room for a while. Rader headed for his place, the Diehard, to see how things were going there. After caring for their horses Slade and the sheriff joined him to indulge in coffee and a snort, which they consumed in leisurely comfort.

The sheriff was at the bar, conversing with a couple of owners he knew, and Slade was alone at his table when Lerner entered and sat down. He looked around, lowered his voice.

"Walt," he said, "there's something I think you should

89

know. May not mean anything to you, but then again it may. Fact is, I feel it will. Day after tomorrow, the Stockton stage is going to be diverted to Echo; should get here around day after tomorrow midnight. The move is supposed to be a dead secret, but you know how such things usually are, never as secret as they are intended to be."

"Why secret?" *El Halcón* asked, and had a very good notion what the answer would be. Lerner glanced around again, lowered his voice still more.

"Because," he said impressively, "that stage will be packing a large sum of money, consigned to the well owners, who need it with which to pay wages and meet other obligations. What do you think?"

"I think," Slade replied, "that you did me what might well be a big favor by telling me about it. Plan to arrive here about midnight?"

"That's right," nodded Lerner.

"Which means," Slade said, "that the stage will very likely leave Stockton before daylight and halt someplace for a couple of hours to feed and rest the horses. The trail which continues up the northern slope after crossing the oil-field basin runs but a short distance to the east of Fort Stockton. That's the route they'll follow. This requires a little thought. Could just possibly provide the opportunity I'm very much in need of. Might bring the head devil of the outlaw bunch out into the open for once."

"Walt," Lerner asked, "do you know who is the head of the bunch?"

"I do," Slade replied, and told him who. Lerner whistled under his breath.

"Fred Norton!" he repeated. "You know, for quite a while I've had a funny feeling about that feller. Could hardly say why, but something about him just didn't seem right."

"You're getting to be like Mary," Slade smiled. "She spots 'em first off."

"And you figure they'll come by way of the old Indian trail?" Lerner said.

"Yes," Slade answered. "It isn't much of a trail, but like most of the old Indian tracks, it's direct and bypasses most of the hills and ridges. They'll leave Fort Stockton as if headed for Sanderson, per usual, and after a bit veer to the east."

"And if they do make a try for the money, have you any notion where it'll take place?"

"My guess is it will be in the breaks a few miles to the north of here, where the going is rough and when everybody will be tired and sleepy and less on the alert," Slade said. "Stage will be guarded, of course?"

"Guard on the seat beside the driver, two more locked inside the coach," Lerner replied.

"Regulation procedure," Slade said. "One thing is sure for certain: if an attempt is made it will be in a novel manner, original and unexpected. The hellion has a genius for that."

"And *El Halcón* has a genius for properly taking care of such matters," the oil magnate stated with emphasis. As Tom Crane would say, my money's on *El Halcón*."

"Hope you won't both end up eating snowballs, as the saying goes," Slade laughed.

"Don't think I'd take to a diet of snow, so my money's still on *El Halcón,* the winner, though I do believe my cook could dish up a snowball in a manner to make it palatable," was the cheerful rejoinder. "Here comes Crane, so let's amble over to my place and see what he's got in store for us. Something plumb special, I'll wager, with *El Halcón* the honored guest. Come along, Tom, time to eat. See you later, Rader."

Following the voluble oilman, they soon reached his place, where they found Mary chatting with the cook and his helpers, and all ready to partake of his culinary offerings.

After complimenting the cook by cleaning their plates to the last smidgeon, and with pipe and cigarettes lighted, they discussed at length the information Lerner had given Slade. And *El Halcón* mapped a plan of action.

"If anybody can think of something better, let's have it," he concluded.

There was a general shaking of heads.

"Sounds foolproof to me," said the sheriff. "What do you think, Mary?"

"On with the dance, let joy be unconfined!" the girl

replied. "Which reminds me, I want to dance. Let's go down to the Diehard for a while."

They did, and spent a pleasant evening devoid of untoward incident.

The carts rolled about midmorning. One of the outriders detoured by way of Tumble to summon Deputy Ester to Sanderson. The carts reached the railroad town before sunset and were lined up for loading the following day.

FOURTEEN

Deputy Ester had already reached Sanderson. Crane sent him to round up Deputy Blount and Alf, the old special. They foregathered in the sheriff's office and Slade outlined his plan that he hoped would thwart a possible attempt against the Fort Stockton stage.

"For almost the whole distance from Fort Stockton the old trail runs across open prairie with no very favorable spots to stage a drygulching," he explained. "But about three miles to the north of the Echo basin is that line of breaks and broken ground. If there is a try made, I figure it will be made somewhere in the breaks, where there are plenty of favorable spots. The old Indians knew how to run a straight track, and that trail is no exception.

"And as it happens, there is a not-too-high bridge that parallels the trail for the whole distance through the breaks, from the crest of which the trail is visible for several hundred yards in both directions. On that ridge, at the north edge of the breaks, is where we'll make our stand. When the stage appears, we'll ride the ridge crest parallel to the track and be able to keep the coach in view."

"Sounds good," the sheriff interpolated.

"Yes," Slade said. "Of course we'll be running the risk of being spotted, with unpleasant results where we are concerned, but we'll have to chance that. We should be able to ascertain where the try will be made. On the surface, it seems ridiculous that one will be made, with the guards on the job. But as I said before, if one is made, it will be in a novel and unexpected manner. And I have a hunch, with all the odds against it, one is going to be made."

"And we're all ready at any time to follow one of your hunches," remarked old Alf. The others nodded sober agreement.

"Then we're all set," Slade said. "We'll leave town around the middle of the afternoon, reaching the breaks after dark, which is the safest way. Later there'll be a moon that should provide us with all the light we need to observe what's going on."

"Not going by way of Echo, then," the sheriff remarked.

"That would be a give-away should somebody in Echo be keeping tabs on us there," Slade replied. "We're riding with the carts from Sanderson. Mary is making a quick run to Tumble before the big shipment to Echo. They want mostly casings at Echo, which will arrive here late tomorrow at the earliest, via railroad.

"The move will be to our advantage against the chance the shrewd hellion has somebody stationed here, which I wouldn't put past him. So we'll just take it easy the rest of the day, and tonight, and hope nothing will cut loose to disrupt our plans."

"And it'll soon be time to eat," remarked Crane. "So after we go over the details once more, suppose we amble to the Branding Pen for a surrounding." Which they proceeded to do.

The night passed without misadventure of any kind, which Slade thought would be the case. They enjoyed a leisurely dinner, after which he and Mary had several dances together, paid a short visit to the Hog Wallow, and then sought rest against the hard day in the offing.

With the promise of a bonus in view for fast work, the carters sifted sand and the loads were in place on time. Under the afternoon sun, the carts rolled for Tumble. Slade and his little posse rode with them. For a while he kept a close watch on the back track, decided they were not wearing a tail, and several miles from Sanderson parted company with the cart train, Mary anxiously watching them out of sight.

Slade set a fair pace, not too fast, for they had plenty of time to reach their destination and he wanted the horses to be as fresh as possible before tackling the breaks. He chuckled to himself as he realized he was glancing westward to see if there were any thunderheads towering into the sky. There were not.

The sunset flamed, the dark closed down, and finally they saw the breaks, grim and ominous against the stars.

Crossing the open prairie was a rather ticklish business, but nothing happened, and before long found them at the base of the ridge. The slope was not difficult for the cayuses to negotiate. They crossed the wooded crest, and at the base of the far slope, which was not very steep, the old trail lay before them.

As Slade said, the visibility was good in both directions for several hundred yards. They stationed themselves close to where the trail from the north entered the breaks and resigned themselves to wait.

An hour passed, the better part of another, and the moon peeped over the horizon and soon was flooding the scene with silvery light.

"Keep your voices down," *El Halcón* warned. "No telling just where the devils are holed up, if they are here, and it's best not to take chances with such a bunch. Norton is uncanny in his ability to size up a situation."

Another hour passed, and midnight was not far off. Slade began to wonder a little were they on a fool's errand; started to look a little that way.

But his hunch persisted, in fact grew strong as time passed. And finally he sighted the coach, lumbering down from the north. The posse tensed for action.

The clumsy vehicle passed beneath them and rolled on, with the posse keeping pace, Slade scanning the terrain in every direction, studying the trail and its environs.

Abruptly he sighted something that held his attention. Directly ahead, a big tree leaned across the track, an unusual position. What the devil? Blazes! The thing was moving! He jerked Shadow to a halt, the others crowding behind him.

The stage was but a few paces from the tree when there was a sharp crack and down it rushed. The massive trunk crashed on top of the stage, its branches thrashing. The terrified horses spun around from the frightful sound and cramped the wheels.

Over went the coach on its side. The driver and the outside guard were hurled from their high perch like peas from a shooter, to thud into the low bush that flanked the far side of the trail.

And out of the growth at the base of the slope bulged six horsemen, shooting at the overturned coach.

"Let them have it!" Slade thundered, shooting with both

hands as he sent Shadow surging down the slope, the posse blazing away beside him.

But the outlaws, caught utterly by surprise as they were, fought back with desperate courage. It was quite dark at the base of the slope, the pale moonglow lighted only by the flame of the guns. It was a battle royal in the shadowy gloom. A slug ripped through Slade's shirtsleeve, another creased the leg of his overalls. By the flash of his Colts he saw that three of the drygulchers were down. He lined sights and a fourth fell.

Again that high, musical, but amazingly penetrating voice blared a command. The two robbers still in their hulls streaked north. And at that instant the demoralized stage horses finally tore loose from the coach and the posse was engulfed in their wild tangle. Ester's mount was knocked off its feet, the deputy sprawled beside the dead outlaws. The cayuse regained its feet just in time to barge into Shadow and was knocked down again, but threw the great black off balance for a moment and Slade scored two misses in consequence.

And by that time the fleeing robbers were but blobs in the distance. Trying to catch up with them before they found sanctuary in some thicket or gulley was out of the question.

The driver and the outside guard, bruised and scratched and bleeding, came floundering from the brush. From inside the coach came muffled yells, their vigor giving proof that the two imprisoned guards were not seriously injured.

Slade let loose another roar to still the tumult.

"Quiet! Everything under control. Open the upper door and come out."

"Can't," came the reply. "Blankety-blank door is jammed."

With a mutter of disgust, Slade seized the handle, put forth his great strength, and tore it open.

One of the guards came scrambling out, under his arm a plump money pouch. The other lingered a moment.

"A lantern in here if it ain't busted," he said.

Evidently it was not, for there was the flicker of a struck match, then a soft glow.

"Anybody hurt?" the Ranger asked anxiously.

Deputy Blount was bleeding slightly from a bullet-scraped arm; old Alf was bleeding even less from a crease across the back of his hand. Deputy Ester had a sizable bump on the side of his head. Slade's leg was barely grained, and the sheriff was untouched.

"Which is a lot better than I had hoped for at one time," Slade said thankfully.

"The way you planned it paid off," said the sheriff. "They were plumb surprised and shot wild. How in blazes did they manage to drop that blankety-blank tree on top of the coach?"

"Trunk sawed almost through, with the tree having a slight natural lean across the trail," Slade explained. "Held it up with a prop. That crackling we heard was when they knocked the prop out and let the tree fall. I encountered something somewhat similar once but not handled so cleverly as this time; the tree just dropped in front of the stage. Okay, catch the stage horses—they are down the trail a ways—strip off the broken harness and fashion bridles. Take the rigs off the outlaw cayuses and turn them loose to be picked up later.

The guard with the money pouch shoved it into Slade's hands. "You look after it from now on," he said. "I never want to see the blankety-blank thing again. Because of it, I figured we were all goners."

"And if Mr. Slade hadn't figured everything out right and got the jump on those devils, there's a darn good chance you would have been," the sheriff put in. "A killer bunch, and not much given to leaving witnesses alive." The guard shivered.

By the light of the lantern, Slade and the sheriff examined the bodies of the slain owlhoots. Hard men to the last, they looked it, with their brutal features and even in death a vicious gleam in the glazing eyes.

"And their horses' brands are slick-ironed Arizona burns or I'm greatly mistaken," Slade said. "I've a notion," lowering his voice, "that these are of Norton's original bunch he brought with him from the west."

"Which should mean he's getting sorta short on hired hands, wouldn't you say?" remarked Crane.

"Possibly, but if he can manage to pull a successful raid or two he'll have no trouble recruiting replacements," Slade replied. "Plenty of that sort in this section."

"You're darn right," growled the sheriff. "It's crawlin' with them. What we going to do with the carcasses?"

"We'll have Lerner pack them to Sanderson in a cart," Slade decided. "Well, I see the boys have gotten makeshift bridles on the stage horses, so we might as well head for Echo. When we get to Lerner's place, I'll patch up the scratches; do a better chore there, with more light. All set? Let's go. Lerner will dispatch a crew to repair the stage and it can continue on its belated way to Sanderson. He's already made arrangements for the layover in Echo tonight."

The queer procession jogged on to the oil town. When it arrived, they found Lerner's place lighted and several well owners congregated there, anxiously awaiting the arrival of the stage.

They rejoiced upon learning nobody was seriously injured and thankfully received the money pouch from Slade.

"We were beginning to feel that something bad must have happened," Lerner said. "Guess the community owes you another vote of thanks, Mr. Slade. As I said before, I don't know what the blazes we would do without you."

"Go busted, the chances are," snorted Crane. The well owners departed, still showering Slade with plaudits and thanks. After the horses were cared for, Slade did a little patching up of the minor wounds. By which time a bountiful supply of food was ready for posse and stage crew.

After they had finished eating, Lerner led the stage crew to the quarters prepared for them. Slade and the other members of the posse went to bed.

Slade enjoyed several hours of refreshing sleep, awaking to find the others already astir. **FIFTEEN**

"Figure the head of the bunch was one of the hellions who escaped?" the sheriff asked.

"Undoubtedly," *El Halcón* replied. "I heard his voice again. Seems he always gets a break. I was lining sights with him when the confounded stage horses tangled my twine. By the time I got free from them, he was in the clear."

"Didn't do too bad, though," was Crane's consoling answer. "Saved the money and did for four of the devils, which helps."

"Yes, but so long as he is on the loose we can look for more trouble," Slade said. "Oh well, next time is another time, and perhaps his luck will eventually run out."

"It will, or rather you'll run it out," said the sheriff, confidently. "Now what's in order?"

Slade pondered for a few minutes, glanced at the clock.

"After some coffee and a bite to eat, we'll head for Tumble," he replied. "Mary won't roll her empties to Sanderson until she gets some sort of a report from us. We'll decide whether to accompany the carts to Sanderson or not after we reach Tumble."

"A good notion," said Crane. "No sense in holding the gal biting her nails."

They enjoyed a leisurely breakfast, there being no great hurry, and then set out for the oil town. Slade veered the course a little to the east and they followed the railroad across Blake's and Kerr's land.

Several times Slade paused to study some curve that detoured a patch of marshy ground, or to inspect a bridge thrown across a narrow ravine. He was satisfied with all he saw.

Once he turned to gaze west by north toward where he knew cranky old Nate Chambrun's *casa* was located. Chambrun was still a problem.

Tumble was busy and boisterous, per usual. Mary was greatly relieved when they showed up safe and sound, and didn't hesitate to say so. She had her empties all set to roll for Sanderson, and after a few minutes of deliberation, Slade decided to accompany the train.

Mary was given a detailed account of the previous night's stirring happenings, the sheriff doing most of the talking, with the deputies putting in a word now and then, Slade listening resignedly.

"To hear them tell it, I was there by myself," he said when the others paused for breath. "As it happened, fortunately for me, they were there, too."

"Never a dull moment in your company," Mary said, shaking her curly head at him. "Well, you are all back safe save for a few scratches, and as I believe I've said before, that's what really counts."

Outside, Saxon, the head carter, cut loose with a couple of impatient whoops.

"Okay, we're coming," Mary called. "Let 'em amble."

The train got under way and continued without interruption, arriving at the railroad town shortly after dark. The carts were placed in loading position, the critters cared for. The deputies departed in search of food and other refreshment. Mary retired to her room for a while. Slade and the sheriff repaired to the office to talk things over.

They had been there but a short period when Lerner's cart containing the dead outlaws arrived. The bodies were carried inside and placed on the floor, where Crane regarded them with satisfaction.

"Yes, floor looks so much better when decorated proper," he declared. "Guess we'd better look 'em over before folks get wind of the fact they're here and barge in pestering us with questions."

He locked the door and drew the window blind and got busy.

The owlhoot pockets divulged nothing of interest save a good deal of money, which Crane stowed in his office safe.

"But not so much as the others coughed up," he said. "Guess losing out on a few good hauls is beginning to hurt."

"Without doubt," Slade agreed. "Which means trouble

100

in the offing. He needs to replenish his exchequer and will be planning something. Now if we can just anticipate what he has in mind."

"You've done a good chore of anticipating of late," the sheriff commented. "I'm looking forward to more of the same brand. That's my hunch."

"Hope it's a straight one," Slade smiled. "Well, suppose we head for the Branding Pen and a helping before folks begin to drop in. Mary will meet us there. The deputies will take over here as soon as they finish eating."

"A good notion," Crane agreed. "I hanker for a snort or two; been quite a while since I had one. Let's amble."

When they entered the Branding Pen, the carters, already at the bar, whooped a greeting and voiced a willingness to back up Hardrock's threat to whack a curious skull or two if Slade and the sheriff were bothered before they finished eating.

With coffee and a snort, they waited for Mary to join them, which she did shortly, dressed for dancing.

"But right now I'm starving," she declared. Slade beckoned a waiter. The kitchen door opened as he approached with their orders, and the cook and his helpers bowed to *El Halcón* and waved a greeting, which they returned.

The cook had evidently anticipated, for very soon their food was before them, and pronounced excellent.

"Doc Cooper wants to hold an inquest on those carcasses in about a half-hour from now," said the sheriff, pushing back his empty plate and hauling out his pipe. "So after we finish our smoke, we might as well amble to the office and get the darn foolishness over with."

"I'll wait for you here," Mary said. "Then a couple of dances and call it an early night. I hardly slept last night, and there's work to do tomorrow."

The deputies were in the office when Slade and the Sheriff reached it. As were a few of the curious, peering at the bodies, voicing vague conjectures. According to the deputies, nobody could recall ever seeing the owlhoots before.

The inquest was brief, the wording of the verdict monotonously similar to others that had gone before. The deceased met their death at the hands of law-enforcement officers performing their duty. Plant 'em and forget 'em.

Back at the Branding Pen, Mary had her dances, the sheriff an extra snort, and everybody did call it a night.

The following morning, Slade and the sheriff again sat in the office discussing the situation and endeavoring, vainly, to figure just where Norton and his hellions were most likely to strike.

"And I'm of the opinion that once more it will be in a novel and unexpected manner," Slade said.

"Oh, I suppose so," grumbled the sheriff. "As you said, the sidewinder has a genius for such things."

"And I'll tell you what I'm going to do," Slade said. "Put *Señor* Norton out of my mind for the time being and concentrate on something else."

"And what's that?" Crane asked.

"I'm riding to the railroad and look things over there," Slade told him. "The steel is getting close to Nate Chambrun's Forked N holding, should reach it in a few more days, and I still don't know what to do about that old coot."

"Hadn't I better go with you?" Crane suggested.

"Really I don't think it necessary," Slade replied. "I'll be on the open prairie and safe enough. You keep an eye on things here and make sure Mary gets her chore of loading finished so she can roll for Echo tomorrow."

"Okay," the sheriff agreed dubiously. "Watch your step."

Slade promised to do so.

Reaching Shadow's stable, he cinched up and mounted. "A little leg stretching for you," he told the big black. "So stop complaining."

Shadow, who liked leg stretching, gave vent to a derisive snort and ambled on.

Slade rode at a fair pace, pondering the problem that confronted him, endeavoring to build up an argument that might appeal to stubborn old Nate Chambrun, without much luck. Began to look like it would be necessary to invoke Eminent Domain. Which, Slade felt, would mean that he had fallen down on the job, and that Jaggers Dunn would be disappointed.

He was riding across Gird Blake's Square and Circle spread, and not far south of Chambrun's Forked N holding, when his old *amigo* Fate decided to really take a hand.

Perhaps five hundred yards ahead was a stretch of chaparral. And suddenly from behind that stretch came a crackle of shots. Slade straightened in the saddle and stared, hand instinctively dropping to the butt of his Winchester snugged in the saddle boot.

Around the south end of the chaparral bulged a horseman, spurring and quirting, bending low in the hull. Another moment and three more riders barged into view, shooting at the lone horseman.

Abruptly he straightened in the saddle, lurched sideways, and fell, to lie writhing and twitching.

The pursuers whooped with triumph. One gave a startled yelp and they began pouring lead in Slade's direction, the slugs buzzing past the Ranger like angry hornets.

That was too much! Slade whipped the Winchester from the boot, clamped it to his shoulder, and returned the fire.

The distance was rather great, but not great enough to handicap the fastest and most accurate gunhand in the whole Southwest. One of the pursuers spun from his hull to lie motionless. Slade shifted the muzzle of the big rifle a fraction and squeezed the trigger.

A second gunslinger fell. The one remaining jerked his horse around and streaked back the way he had come, bending low, flogging his mount.

Slade let him go. He didn't know what it was all about, and without doubt the man writhing and jerking on the ground was urgently in need of attention. Slade sent Shadow racing ahead. Reaching the wounded man, he left the saddle with Shadow skating to a halt.

One glance told him that there was not a moment to spare if the fellow's life were to be saved. He had been shot through the left shoulder and blood was gushing from the wound.

When he whipped his medicants from the saddle pouch and knelt beside the helpless form, he saw he was a young fellow, little more than a boy.

His sensitive fingers quickly located the exact spot to apply pressure, and almost at once the flow of blood appreciably lessened.

"Can you hear me?" he asked.

"Yes," the boy gasped.

"Bring your right arm across your chest and put your

thumb right where I have mine. That's right—press—press hard. It'll hurt, but if we don't get that blood flow stopped you'll be dead in five minutes. Good! You're doing fine! Hold it right that way."

Working at top speed, he quickly had the wound heavily padded on both sides, the pads bandaged into place. He gazed at the slight stain showing on the bandage, applied still another strip, drawn tight, and nodded with satisfaction.

"That should hold you," he said. "Now just relax and take it easy for a while."

As he spoke, he rolled and lighted a cigarette and put it between the boy's quivering lips. A couple of deep drags and the quivering lessened. His eyes lost some of the wildness of expression that had glazed them.

"G-guess if it wasn't for you, I'd been a goner," he gasped, trying hard to smile.

"Who are you, and where do you belong?" Slade asked.

"I'm Webb Chambrun," the boy answered, his voice something like normal. "Nate Chambrun, who owns the Forked N spread, is my grandfather."

"I see," Slade said. "And why were those fellows shooting at you?"

"I haven't the slightest notion," the boy returned. "They just started shooting when they saw me."

"Okay, we'll take that up later," Slade said. "Your horse didn't stray. I'll get the rig off and turn it loose to be picked up later. We can't bother with it now."

The chore was quickly finished. Slade picked up the boy's slight form, cradled it against his breast, and turned to Shadow.

"Don't move," he told his burden. "Let me get into the hull."

"Do—do you think you can do it?" the boy asked. Slade smiled, put one foot in the stirrup, slowly stood erect, and swung his other leg across the saddle, his other foot into the stirrup.

"All set to go," he said. "I know where your *casa* is located. Just take it easy."

The distance they had to cover was not great, for which Slade was grateful. He didn't think the slight jolting would start the bleeding afresh, but there was always the chance it might. Less than half an hour later they rode into the ranchhouse yard.

Big old Nate Chambrun was sitting on the porch. He had bold features and truculent eyes. He surged to his feet.

"What the hell!" he bawled.

"He's shot," Slade tersely answered as he dismounted, the boy still cradled against his breast.

"Did you shoot him?" Chambrun demanded.

"Hush, Grandpa!" the boy panted. "Of course he didn't shoot me. He saved my life and killed two of the devils that did shoot me."

"What—what—" Chambrun began.

"Hold your questions." Slade snapped. "Get a couch ready on which to place him. And send a rider to Sanderson to fetch Doctor Cooper and Sheriff Crane. Move!"

The last word blared at the rancher like a gunshot. He moved! Bellowing orders that brought a couple of wranglers into the yard. Slade carried the boy into the living room of the big house, where an old Mexican, the cook, was already spreading sheets and blankets on a couch. He bowed low to *El Halcón,* who voiced a Spanish greeting. Very quickly they had the wounded boy comfortable. A clatter of hoofs outside told that a rider was heading for Sanderson.

"Say!" Chambrun exclaimed. "You must be Slade, Crane's special deputy. I've heard things about you."

"And I've heard things about you, and I'm inclined to believe they're true," Slade replied. "That you are an opinionated, narrow-minded, arrogant, stubborn, selfish, pigheaded old coot with no use for progress of any kind, interested solely in your own convenience and desires, with no thought of others."

That was just the beginning. He proceeded to give Chambrun such a tongue lashing as he had never experienced in his long life.

"And there," he concluded, pointing to the boy on the couch, "is an example of what your attitude can bring about. You must feel very good about it."

The searing contempt in the last words turned Chambrun red, then turned him white as the Terrible Eyes of *El Halcón* beat hard on his face.

"Maybe you're right, maybe I did wrong," he said

105

heavily. "Anyhow, Slade, I'm mighty, mighty beholden to you. He's all I've got in the world."

Tears stole down the wrinkled old face.

And abruptly Slade smiled, the flashing white smile of *El Halcón,* with the little devils of laughter in the depths of his cold eyes dancing gaily to the front. And old Nate looked like he all of a sudden felt warm inside.

"Feller," he said, "if there's any way I can do you a favor, big or little, I don't care what, just tell me and it's yours for the asking."

"Well," Slade smiled, "you can do me a little one and a big one. The little one? A cup of coffee."

Chambrun hurried to the kitchen to order the coffee. "Mig," he said to the old cook, "you seem to know him."

"Yes, *patrón,* I know him," the cook replied. "He is *El Halcón! El Halcón* the good, the just, the compassionate, the friend of the lowly. Fear not, *patrón,* young Webster will not die. *El Halcón* bound up his wounds, and *El Halcón's* touch is the touch of the Great Physician. Webster will not die."

"Mig," Chambrun said, "I believe you're right." He carried in the coffee himself.

"And the big favor?" he prompted.

"That you stop your senseless opposition to the railroad and let it cross your land without hindrance."

"I'll do it," Chambrun promised without an instant's hesitation.

"Thank you, sir," Slade acknowledged. "And I venture to predict that eventually the coming of the railroad will work to your advantage."

"If you say so, I guess it will," Chambrun admitted.

Slade took time out to examine his patient and found the pads and bandages in satisfactory condition, the boy breathing easier.

"A couple more pillows, prop him up, and give him hot coffee, all he wants," he said. "He's lost a good deal of blood and the coffee will help."

After the chore was cared for and young Webb was sipping the hot liquid and smiling wanly, Slade added, "And send somebody to retrieve his horse, and the outlaw horses if they can be located; I don't think they ran far."

"And what about the two dead men, how about sending my little wagon along to pack them in and stash them in the barn?" Chambrun suggested.

"That will be good," Slade replied. "The sheriff will desire to look them over and take them to his office in Sanderson."

"We'll take care of that, too," said Chambrun. He contemplated the boy sipping his coffee, and with now a tinge of color in his cheeks.

"Wonder why they shot Webb?" he remarked.

"Had he been killed, wouldn't you have been inclined to blame the railroad or the oil field?" Slade countered.

"Guess I would have," Chambrun conceded.

"An old story, but it works, all too often," Slade said. "Get two outfits of honest men on the prod against each other, blaming each other for anything untoward that happens, leaving two owlhoots a clear field to operate. Yes, as I've said before, it works."

"It's not going to work any more so far as I'm concerned," Chambrun promised grimly. He went out and gave orders to several hands who were busy around the barn and the horse corral.

"Everything will be taken care of pronto," he reported. "Well, I've a notion you can do with something to eat, after all the excitement, and I believe I can stow away a bite myself."

"I'm in favor of it," Slade agreed. "First, though, I want to care for my horse. He's been standing out there long enough."

"I'll do it," Chambrun offered.

"Okay," Slade answered. "But I'll go along with you and introduce you to him. Otherwise you'll likely lose half your arm if you try to put a hand on him."

"A one-man horse, eh?" Chambrun remarked. "Well, all I've got to say is he shows darn good judgment."

"Thank you," Slade smiled.

Shadow was properly cared for with a full manger of oats. And by that time the cook had food on the table.

Shortly after they finished eating, the wagon rolled in with the bodies. Webb's mount and the outlaw horses were also brought along. The rigs were stripped off and they were placed in the corral.

The dead outlaws were declared mean-looking devils.

Slade reserved judgment until he could give them a more thorough once-over in a better light. He did ascertain from their hands that both had been working punchers a long time back. He refrained from going through their pockets until the sheriff was present.

Now the cowhands were riding in from their work on the range and were also profuse in their thanks to Slade, young Webb being a universal favorite. He had finished his coffee and Slade eased him down from the pillows. Soon he was dozing, which Slade considered a good sign.

It was long past full dark when the sheriff and Doc Cooper arrived. He glanced at the patient, turned to Slade.

"Well, what about it?" he asked.

"Don't see any reason why he shouldn't pull through," the Ranger replied. "He's young, tough as a pine knot, and I doubt if he's ever had a sick day. Lost a bit of blood, but I managed to get the flow stopped. My opinion is he'll make the grade."

"If that's your diagnosis, I'll string along with it," said the doctor. "Never knew you to be wrong. I'll change the bandages and the pads and give him a sedative, and keep an eye on him during the night. I'll sleep on that couch the other side of the room. Now Tom and I can go for a snort or two and a surrounding. And Nate, you can thank your lucky stars that Slade happened along when he did. Otherwise you'd be short a grandson."

"Don't I know it!" sighed Chambrun.

"More floor decorations, eh?" the sheriff observed to Slade. "Yes, Mary got her carts rolling on time. Should be in Echo by now."

"Think I'll ride to Echo tomorrow, after stopping at the railhead for a word with Broderick, the engineer," Slade said.

"And if Nate sends the carcasses to Sanderson in his wagon, where Blount and Ester will receive them, I'll ride with you, if you don't mind," replied the sheriff. "Well, you've sure got yourself in solid with Chambrun. He worships the kid, whose mother and father, Nate's son, were killed in a fire a few years back. You won't have any more trouble with Nate."

Later when they had a chance to be alone for a few minutes, Chambrun asked Doc Cooper a question.

"Just what is he, John? I never met anybody like him before."

The doctor spoke slowly. "A man who could be high in the seats of the mighty, but who has the audacity to fling material things to the winds in his search after ideals."

Old Nate bowed his head.

Walt Slade went to sleep that night firmly convinced that Fate, or something, had certainly lent a hand.

Crane examined the bodies the following **SIXTEEN**
morning and agreed with the wrangler's
comment that they were mean-looking devils. He extracted
some money from their pockets; they were loaded into
Chambrun's little wagon and went trundling on their way.

"Think they were some of Norton's original bunch?"
the sheriff asked Slade.

"Couldn't say for sure, but the brands their horses
wear are undoubtedly Arizona slick-ironed burns," Slade
replied.

Doc Cooper decided to remain at the Forked N ranchhouse another day to observe Webb's improvement and
to instruct the competent old cook how to minister to the
convalescent. Slade said good-bye to everybody and he
and the sheriff headed for the railhead.

"Didn't get much money off the hellions this time,"
Crane remarked. "Guess the head devil is scraping the
bottom of the barrel, with trouble in the offing for us."

"My opinion," Slade agreed. "Yes, here we go again!"

"Well, you've sure been doing all right so far," Crane
chuckled.

Without incident they reached the railhead, which was
nearing Chambrun's holding, with Broderick decidedly
worried over what might be ahead.

"Just keep right on driving steel," Slade told him.
"Nothing to worry about. You'll meet with no opposition
from Chambrun. We had a little talk and he agreed to be
reasonable."

"I don't know how you do it! I don't know how you do
it!" sighed Broderick.

Not a very original remark where *El Halcón* was concerned, others having voiced similar bewildered comments.

"You have but one hard chore ahead of you, driving
the cut through the hills to the oil-field basin," Slade
resumed. "And that shouldn't be too hard. Fortunately,
the hills to the south are much lower than those on the
other three sides of the bowl, and I think the soil is
mostly earth. Your shovels should make short work of
that. And you are making excellent progress. Mr. Dunn

will be very pleased. Okay, the sheriff and I are heading for Echo. Be seeing you soon."

They rode on, leaving Broderick smiling happily, climbed the slope by way of the old Indian trail, crossed the crest and down the far sag to the field, a scene of even greater activity than on the occasion of their last visit.

For now two big storage tanks were completed, two more on the way; and with plenty of casings brought in via Mary's carts, the walking beams were again creaking and jigging, the drill bits thudding.

Lerner met them and was overjoyed at the news that the railroad was booming ahead apace and that before a great deal more time had passed, the field would be provided with the sorely needed tank cars.

After stabling their horses, Slade and the sheriff made their way to where Mary's carts were almost unloaded.

"Well, let's have it," the girl said after greeting Slade with a kiss, the twinkle-eyed sheriff with a grimace. "I know very well you've been mixed up in something."

They told her, Crane doing the most of the telling. She shook her curly head resignedly.

"I've said it so many times it has become downright monotonous," she declared. "Let you out of my sight and you're into something. Oh, well, I guess I'm one of those that never learn, but I am glad to see you. Now sift sand, I've work to do. We'll all have dinner in Mr. Lerner's place, and maybe I'll be able to relax in peace tonight and enjoy myself a little. Be seeing you."

The sheriff announced his intention of visiting with Vince Rader at the Diehard for a while. Slade decided to walk around town, look things over, and think a little.

Although greatly pleased at being able to iron out the railroad's difficulties, he was far from satisfied with the situation as it stood. Fred Norton and his owlhoots were very much on the loose, and Slade experienced an unpleasant premonition that they were due to strike someplace soon. With always the grim probability that some innocent person would die. The devils were utterly ruthless and thought no more of killing a man than of swatting a fly. Witness the attack on young Webb Chambrun.

What to do about it? He'd be hanged if he knew at the moment. He gazed morosely at the glory of the sunset flaming behind the hills, feeling regretfully that he could not really appreciate its beauty properly with so much on his mind.

Finally he gave it up in disgust and entered the Diehard, where he found Rader and the sheriff well fortified with glasses and in a jovial mood.

"Tom was telling me how you saved young Chambrun's life," Rader said. "It was a wonderful thing you did, Mr. Slade, and also it would appear it got you and old Nate together. Which is good for all of us here in the field. Strange how things work out."

"Yes, often good comes from evil, if we will just recognize the fact," Slade replied.

"Yes, no doubt of that, although at times it's hard to see how it could. Guess we just have to have faith," Rader said.

"Exactly," *El Halcón* answered.

Lerner dropped in to announce that dinner would be ready very shortly.

"And the other day I got to thinking about something," he said. "I just was wondering why the ranchers never tried to stop the carts passing over their land. Wouldn't it look like they would have?"

Slade shook his head.

"That old track the carts follow is an open trail," he explained. "And you can't block an open trail and get away with it. Not in Texas."

"I see," nodded Lerner. "Well, let's go eat. Be seeing you, Rader."

Happy is the man who, by reason of good fortune, knows not the meaning of the word hunger. But still happier is he who, when the hand of famine pinches, may stave his craving with such a meal as Westbrook Lerner's old cook dished up that night.

So Walt Slade thought, and he and the others consumed the repast in the silence that is the fitting tribute to tasty food.

"And now," said Mary, "I'm going to my room and rest a while. I just remembered that I've been up since the crack of dawn, and with very little sleep before that, with you two gallivanting around somewhere."

"Build up your strength," counseled the sheriff. "Build up your strength."

Mary made a face at him and flounced up to her room.

"A couple of snorts and I'm fit for anything," said Crane. "What do you think, Walt?"

"I wish I knew what the devil to think," Slade replied wearily. "The more I try to, the less headway I seem to make."

"You'll end up making plenty," the sheriff predicted cheerfully. "No doubt in my mind as to that."

"Here's hoping," Slade said. "Well, as soon as I finish my cigarette, I'm going to take another stroll and look things over. I'll meet you and Westbrook and Mary at the Diehard. Okay?"

"Watch your step," cautioned the sheriff. "No telling what may happen out there in the dark."

A few minutes later, Slade departed, wandering along the busy streets.

The town was growing fast. Now there were three more saloons, a couple more shops, big ones. The building was chiefly to the east, away from the field, where there were few people on the streets, the near or half-finished structures dark and deserted. They would be a hive of activity with the break of day.

Gradually he worked that way. He could always think best in the open air, and under the glitter of the stars and a soft breeze whispering by, his problem appeared less insurmountable. In his mind a plan was in embryo that he believed might work.

Now he was passing a row of dark buildings, most of them about half finished. There was nobody on the street, and somehow those gloomy structures seemed to voice a soundless threat. It was a spooky environment.

A slight sound, as of softly planted boot heels, reached his keen ears. He glanced over his shoulder and saw that, something less than a hundred yards distant, three men were stealing along in his rear, walking purposefully.

"Getting ready to play games, eh?" *El Halcón* murmured. "Okay with me." He glanced ahead and saw something he liked not one bit.

Advancing toward him were three more furtive individuals, and *El Halcón* at once understood. The idea was to catch him in a deadly crossfire.

Slade did some very fast thinking. There was no opening into which he could slip. The glassless windows of the building he was passing were boarded up to keep out the

113

rain. And as he glanced in a vain search for any sanctuary, no matter how dubious, he saw something that caused his pulses to leap exultantly.

The outer sheathing was not yet in place and the transverse beams to which it would be nailed formed, for an active man, a good ladder to the flat roof of the building.

He was halfway up to the roof before the killers realized what he had in mind. There was a torrent of curses, then a blaze of guns, bullets whistling past.

But moving fast and in the shadow, he was an elusive target and none of the slugs found a mark. Another moment and he was over the edge of the roof unharmed.

Nearby was a stack of lumber, into the shadow of which he dived, peering and listening.

Almost immediately he heard a scraping and scuffling at the front of the building. The devils, mad with the blood lust, were storming his position. He unsheathed both Colts and waited.

For what seemed an eternity of crawling suspense he waited. Then abruptly a man's head and shoulders loomed above the edge of the roof, and the flame of a gun, the slug fanning Slade's face. His big Colt boomed. There followed a gasping cry as the man vanished from sight, and a thud. One down!

But almost instantly two more heads appeared, and the cracking of two more guns, sending splinters into Slade's face, ripping his shirtsleeve, smacking the stack of lumber. He fired with both hands as fast as he could squeeze trigger.

Another cry, and two more thuds. A volley of curses, and the pad of running feet, and in the distance, shouts, drawing nearer.

Slade risked the chance that some of the devils had circled the building and were waiting for him. He leaped to his feet, sped to the back of the building, and fairly slid down the ladder formed by the transverse beams. On the ground he crouched low, peering and listening, guns ready for instant action.

However, there was no sign of movement, no sound save of the shouts drawing still nearer. The shooting had been heard, of course, and somebody was coming to investigate. He waited another moment, then slipped into the deserted street on which the building backed, quickly made his way to the corner, halted to peer again. Nobody in sight.

He turned the corner, turned a second one, slowed his pace, and strolled around a third, which was close to the oil field and no great distance from the Diehard saloon.

Here there were plenty of people on the street, exclaiming, questioning, conjecturing, staring eastward, some walking cautiously in that direction.

Slade listened to their chatter for a while, hearing nothing he considered significant, and made his way to the Diehard, where he was greeted with accusing glares.

"Out of my sight a minute!" Mary stormed.

"Where are the carcasses?" asked the sheriff.

"Please, Mr. Slade, tell us what did happen," begged Lerner. "We're eaten up with curiosity."

Slade told them. "I sure got a break in that building with the transverse beams minus sheathing, and happening to be right beside it when I was," he concluded.

"Uh-huh, and with you having the wit to take advantage of it like you did," commented Crane. "Hellions were sure out to get you, and came darn close to doing so, I'd say."

"They were stupid, trying to smoke me out of my hole-up on the roof," Slade said. "Always the little slips."

At that moment an excited man came rushing in, stared about, shouted loudly for the sheriff, and was directed to the table.

"Sheriff," he gabbled, "there are three dead men over on Park Avenue. Looks like they mighta had a falling out and gunned each other."

"That so?" replied Crane. "Okay, I'll go over there. Park Avenue to the east?"

"You all coming along?" he asked his companions.

"I'm staying right where I am," Mary declared with emphasis. "I don't get any pleasure from looking at such things. Mr. Rader will keep me company."

Reaching the building that had proved Slade's salvation, they pushed through the crowd to where the three bodies lay. Slade was willing to agree with the sheriff that they were hard-case devils. Their hands showed they had once been cow punchers, a long time back.

"And I'll wager that when you locate their horses they will be wearing slick-ironed Arizona brands," he told

115

Crane. "More of the original bunch, I'd say. Seems there is no end to them."

Crane nodded gloomy agreement. "Some of you gents pack 'em to Mr. Lerner's stable and lay 'em out," he said. The chore was quickly taken over.

"And search for the three unclaimed horses tomorrow," Slade added; "they'll need to be relieved of their rigs and fed."

Lerner promised to do so.

"And I'm going along with the bodies to see they are properly placed," he announced. "See you at the Diehard."

"Okay," the sheriff said. "We'll look 'em over more closely in the morning. And, Walt, guess we'd better amble back to the Diehard before Mary concludes we've gotten into something else she won't approve."

Mary admitted she was surprised and relieved. Wearied by the excitement and with a hard day ahead, they again called it an early night.

The following morning Slade had a **SEVENTEEN**
talk with Westbrook Lerner. The oil-
man chuckled more than once as Slade outlined what he
had in mind.

"And you feel sure you can persuade Chambrun to go
along with it?" he asked when the Ranger paused.

"No doubt in my mind," Slade replied.

Lerner chuckled some more. "Okay," he said. "I'll get
busy and make preparations. Just wait till the boys see!"

Slade accompanied the empty carts from Echo, but he
soon turned off and headed for Nate Chambrun's Forked
N *casa,* where he received a warm welcome from both
Chambrun and young Webb, who was sitting up in a
chair and looking fine.

Old Nate chuckled even more than had Lerner when
Slade recounted his conversation with the oil tycoon.

"Slade, you beat all!" he chortled. "You told me the
oil field would sooner or later be to my advantage, and
now you go ahead and prove it. No long drive to jolt the
fat off the critters! No transportation costs! No buyers'
commissions! Sure I'll do it; I'd be loco not to."

Slade continued to Sanderson, but he was back in
Echo late the following afternoon.

Meanwhile a trail herd was rolling north, the sun
glinting on horns, smoldering shaggy backs, the cows complaining peevishly.

They complained even more bitterly as they were shoved
up the steep slope, via the old Indian trail, over the burned-
out crest, down the far sag, and into the makeshift corral
Lerner had hastily thrown together.

"Yes, the boys have been bellerin' about a shortage of
meat," he chuckled. "Guess this will shut them up for
a while. I've got Chambrun's money all ready for him.
Top market price, and I'll take your word as to the
weights. Trust you more to get it right than the scale.
Yep, we won't lack for meat for a while.

"Incidentally, I thought you'd want to know, Norton
rode out of town this morning, headed north by west
when he left here. I don't think he's back."

Which was disturbing news for Slade. He wondered what the canny devil was up to. Well, chances are he would learn soon enough, and the learning very probably wouldn't be pleasant. There was little doubt in Slade's mind but that he was up to something. What? There was the rub; Slade hadn't the slightest idea.

And then, as he and Lerner were getting ready for bed, inspiration came to his rescue. He slept soundly for several hours, arose in the dark and still hour before the dawn, dressed quietly, and hurried to Lerner's stable, where Shadow was stalled. He got the rig on the big black, led him out and mounted without disturbing the keeper. Confident he would not be observed in this ungodly hour, he rode north.

"Yes, horse," he told Shadow, "right along I've been missing a bet. Another case of overlooking the obvious because it is so darned obvious. All of a sudden it came to me that Norton and his hellions must have a hangout where they can get together, plan their raids, and divide the loot.

"Where? Where else but in that long and wide stretch of breaks to the north of town. Yes, that's it, no doubt in my mind. So we'll go have a look-see. If we can locate the hangout, we may be able to set a trap for that ambitious gent."

He knew that there were more than one small cabin tucked away in the area, snug against Indian raids in the days when the red man rode, built by hunters or trappers in the time when the section was noted for pelts. In one of those cabins, if he could locate the cabin, might be what he sought. He rode on, slowly, with the breaks steadily drawing nearer.

The false dawn fled across the sky like a ghostly wraith, and all the world was dark.

But not for long. In the east a soft glow birthed, pale rose that brightened to tremulous gold, then deepened to scarlet. Shafts of light stabbed the zenith. The rim of the sun peeped over the horizon, and it was day.

Slade always had staple provisions stowed in his saddle pouches, plus a helping of oats for Shadow. He found a spot where there was grass, and a little spring bubbling up through the loam. Here he set about preparing his breakfast, confident that the trickle of smoke from his tiny fire of dry wood, blending with the morning mists, would not be noticed.

Soon coffee was bubbling in a little flat bucket, bacon and eggs sizzling in a small skillet. Which, with bread, took care of all innermost needs.

After he finished eating and had cleaned and stowed the utensils, he stretched out with a cigarette and watched Shadow meditatively chewing his oats. Now the sun was well up in the sky and he cinched up and set out on his quest, watchful and alert, for there was no telling what might be holed up in the hills, although he was of the opinion that there was nobody. He was convinced that Norton and his devils were off on some foray, about which he would no doubt hear in the near future.

Hour after hour he combed the gulleys, the chaparral stands, the dry washes and shallow canyons, of which there were many. He constantly scanned the sky for that telltale of human presence, smoke, his sensitive nostrils attuned to the possibility that a fire might have been kindled not long ago, the dank smell of recent burning lingering in the air.

Twice he spotted old cabins, neither productive of results, having evidently been abandoned years before.

It was around midafternoon when he found what he sought. He had entered a narrow canyon, not much more than a crack between tall cliffs, when he scented the undoubted odor of stale smoke. Somebody had kindled a fire in the canyon a short time before.

Slade's caution redoubled. He slowed Shadow's pace to a walk and rode with every nerve at hairtrigger alertness.

He had covered a couple of hundred yards or so when directly ahead, the canyon curved sharply. Slade reined in and sat gazing and listening.

"Anyhow, I'm not going to risk your clumping around that bend," he whispered to Shadow. "Into the brush with you, and keep quiet."

Very quickly he had the horse out of sight. With a final glance around, he stole ahead on foot, rounded the bend, and halted. Set against one side wall of the gorge, almost hidden by tall and thick chaparral, was a small cabin. It was evidently very old and weatherbeaten but tight enough to provide shelter from the elements.

For long moments he stood peering and listening, gradu-

119

ally becoming convinced that the old shack was empty so far as human tenancy was concerned. He resolved to take a chance and sped across the little cleared space with quick, light steps, hands close to his guns. He reached the door, flung it open, and uttered an exclamation of satisfaction; he had found Fred Norton's hidden hangout.

Against the walls were bunks covered with blankets. There were a table and several chairs, all homemade. On shelves were stacks of provisions, below them sacks of horse provender.

Sunk in one wall were a fireplace of stone blocks, fire-wood, a bucket of water on the hearth, and a number of cooking utensils. He peered into the fireplace and saw that in its ceiling was a sizable hole which evidently reached the outer air a hundred feet and more above, a convenient chimney that would keep the room free from smoke. All in all, a very comfortable hideaway.

Well, he had found it; all he needed now was an opportunity to put his knowledge to use.

He crossed to the door, absentmindedly conning over what he had learned, shoved it open, and stepped out. And despite all his former care, that moment of abstraction very nearly cost him his life.

Just rounding the bend was a horseman. He uttered a startled exclamation and went for his holster, whipping out a gun with lightning speed.

Slade's draw was a flicker of movement. The two guns blazed almost as one. *El Halcón* stood firm, but the horse-man reeled sideways and fell, to lie motionless, a bullet hole between his fixed and staring eyes.

Strung for instant action, Slade stood gazing toward the bend, but quickly decided the fellow had been alone. He conned over the situation as it stood.

The body must be disposed of, and the horse, which had run a few paces and halted, looking back inquiringly.

Searching about, Slade found a crevice some six or seven feet deep into which he dropped the body, giving the vicious-looking face but a glance. He jammed brush into the crevice, on top of the body. Whistling Shadow, he caught the outlaw horse, bestowing a soothing pat on its neck. He picked up the fellow's fallen gun and tossed it into the crevice. Then he mounted, leading the other animal, and got out of the canyon as fast as he could.

Quickly he reached the open prairie, and after riding west for several hours, he stripped off the lead horse's rig and hid it under a convenient bush.

"You're a good looking critter, despite your slick-iron burn," he told the cayuse. "Somebody will pick you up soon."

Without delay he headed for Sanderson. He was anxious to contact Sheriff Crane and inform him of what he had learned. It was long past full dark when he reached the railroad town, tired, hungry, but exultant, feeling he had accomplished plenty in the course of a busy day. Caring for Shadow, he hurried to the sheriff's office where he found Crane expectant. He was enthusiastic when Slade gave him an account of what he had learned.

"Now all we need is an opportunity to put it to use," he said.

The opportunity would be forthcoming soon, and in an unexpected manner.

"Mary's at the Branding Pen, waiting for you," the sheriff remarked. "She expects to have her carts rolling tomorrow, dependent on whether you showed up tonight or not."

"I hope she's not as hungry as I am," Slade smiled.

"She will be," predicted Crane. "I don't think she eats so well when you're gallivanting. Let's go."

Reaching the Branding Pen, they found Mary relieved—and hungry. The cook got busy without delay.

The Marathon Bank was small, but a go- **EIGHTEEN**
ing concern, for Marathon was the supply
center for the vast ranching country covering the six
thousand square miles of Brewster County, and a lot of
money passed over its counters.

Frequently very large sums came from the El Paso
bank, of which it was a branch, usually via the night
eastbound express that reached Marathon around eleven
o'clock.

The money was received from the express messenger by
two armed guards. They wore uniform jackets and caps
and had deputy sheriffs' badges pinned to the fronts of the
jackets, making them recognizable to the messenger.

That night when Slade, Mary, and the sheriff were
staving off the pangs of hunger, the two guards headed
for the railroad station shortly before eleven. They talked
and laughed together as they walked the quiet and well-
nigh-deserted streets. They were just passing a dark alley
mouth when three men stepped out, and the guards found
themselves looking into the muzzles of guns held by the
three, who had their hatbrims pulled low, their neckerchiefs up high, so that there was little to be seen of their
faces other than their hard, glittering eyes.

The guards knew better than to try to resist, just a
convenient way to commit suicide. They were herded into
the alley, their jackets, caps, and badges stripped off, and
they were securely bound with tie ropes and gagged. Their
captors donned jackets, caps, and badges and stole from
the alley, partially unmasked, leaving the helpless guards
lying on the ground. In the distance sounded the whistle
of the express. After a few moments it ground to a halt.

Confronted by jackets, caps, and badges, the messenger
had no reason to think anything wrong. The money pouch
was handed over, the necessary papers produced from the
jackets, receipts signed. The "guards" said goodnight and
left the station, presumably heading for the bank. The
boom of the locomotive exhaust as the express rolled on
its way drowned the beat of fast hoofs heading east.

Suddenly the bank official waiting to receive the money realized his guards were long overdue. He waited a little longer, then called to the night watchman and they set out for the station, walking fast.

As they passed the dark alley mouth they heard a scuffling and thrashing about. They paused, struck matches to investigate, and found their trussed-up guards. Followed a fair example of Marathon hell. The sheriff of Brewster County was summoned. Telegrams were sent to sheriffs east and west.

He and Slade and Mary were preparing to call it a night when Sheriff Crane received his. A lengthy one, going into details, for Sheriff Chet Traynor of Brewster County believed the robbers were heading for somewhere in the Sanderson area.

"Looks like we may be getting the break we've hoped for," Slade said after reading the message.

"And you figure it was Norton and his bunch?"

"Definitely," Slade replied. "All the earmarks of one of his capers. Take it easy, now, there's no hurry. They won't risk traveling in daylight. They'll hole up somewhere at dawn, plenty of places for anybody familiar with the section, and continue to the cabin in the canyon after nightfall. We'll go along to Echo with Mary and her carts; then some little while after full dark we'll head for the canyon and try and have a nice reception committee all set for the devils when they show.

"I don't think we need fear our movements being spotted, for I am confident that the fellow with whom I shot it out in the canyon was left in Echo to try and keep tabs on us while Norton and the other two, the last of the bunch, pulled the Marathon robbery.

"Let's see now, Deputy Ester is in Tumble. Well, I believe you and I and Deputy Blount should be able to handle the situation. So let's try and get a little rest against a hard night coming up. Okay with everybody?"

After a restful night they assembled in the Branding Pen for a leisurely breakfast. Slade, the sheriff, and Blount wore an expression of pleased expectancy, but Mary's beautiful eyes were somber.

"I only wish I could go with you," she said. "But it is a woman's lot to wait."

"And sometimes I think it is the harder chore," Slade replied gently.

After they finished eating, he went over the details of his plan of operation, making sure his companion knew just what moves to make when the showdown came.

For he believed that the showdown between him and the shrewd elusive Norton was indeed just in the offing. Very likely one or the other of them would not see another sun rise. Well, if your number isn't up on the board, nobody can put it up, so why bother about possibilities. He rolled a cigarette and smoked with carefree enjoyment.

Saxon, the head carter, arrived to announce that the loads were all in place, the carts ready to roll.

Very soon they rolled north and east under sunny skies, the carters hilarious as usual, the outriders fanning out on either side, the little posse bringing up the rear, Mary reining her horse close to Slade's.

Nearing the basin, Slade gazed east at the smoke boiling up from where the steamshovels, the steel following closely, ripped and tore in the last hard chore the railroad builders had to tackle, the driving of the cut through the rise to the town.

"Just a few more days and then the grand opening," he remarked. "Broderick has already wired Mr. Dunn, and I expect him to show up most any time now."

"We'll be here to meet him," the sheriff predicted cheerfully.

"I certainly hope so," sighed Mary.

The carts toiled up the slope, across the crest, and down the far sag to the field, where they received a warm welcome from Lerner and a number of well owners who were profuse in their thanks for the casings and other materials they greatly needed. The unloading began at once.

Slade, Mary, and Blount enjoyed a tasty dinner Lerner's cook put out. Slade went to the kitchen and thanked him for taking such good care of them, leaving him pleased.

For quite some time they smoked and talked over a snort for the sheriff, a glass of wine for Mary. Finally Slade pinched out his last cigarette and glanced at the clock.

"Guess we'd better get going," he said. They departed, again leaving the lonely girl at the table.

Leaving the basin by way of the old Indian trail, they rode north by slightly east. There was no moon as yet, but the sky was brilliant with stars.

As they rode, Slade slipped something from a cunningly concealed secret pocket in his broad leather belt and pinned it to his shirt front. It was a gleaming silver star set on a silver circle, the feared and honored badge of the Texas Rangers.

"The authority it packs sometimes has a good effect," he explained. The others nodded sober understanding.

With his unerring instinct for distance and direction, he led them straight to the mouth of the canyon. Each breathed a little deeper as they entered the gloomy gorge, walking their horses.

It was with some trepidation that Slade approached the bend beyond which the old cabin stood, for there was the chance he might have been mistaken in his belief that Norton and his bunch would not travel during the daylight hours. They could well have already reached the cabin and would hear their approach, with unpleasant results for the posse.

However, the old shack stood silent and dark, to all appearances without occupancy.

"Guessed right, I'd say," he murmured. "We'll shove the horses into the brush over here to the left—plenty of concealment. Then take up our stand opposite the door and wait."

The wait was tedious but not too great. Suddenly they heard hoofbeats beyond the bend. Another moment and three horsemen rode into view. Slade recognized one as the tall, broad-shouldered Frederick Norton.

The three rode straight for the cabin, dismounted, but left the horses standing, still wearing their rigs.

"Not going to stay long, perhaps just long enough to divide the loot," Slade breathed. "We'll wait until they get a light going before we hit them."

Another moment and a light did flare inside the cabin. There was a rumble of voices, a scraping of chair legs on the floor.

"They're sitting down at the table," Slade whispered. "Just another minute, then straight for the door. I'll hit it with my shoulder. Don't take chances, they're killers. All right, let's go!"

Across to the door they sped. Slade hit it with all his two hundred muscular pounds back of his shoulder. It slammed wide open and they were in the cabin.

The three men seated around the table, which was covered with money, surged to their feet.

"Up!" Slade thundered. "I arrest Frederick Norton and others for robbery and murder! In the name of the State of Texas!"

"A blankety-blank Ranger!" Norton screeched. "I might have known it!"

His hand blurred to his gun, but fast as he was, he wasn't quite fast enough. Slade drew and shot before he could squeeze trigger. Again, and still again! The cabin rocked and quivered to the bellow of the guns as Crane and Blount shot it out with the two remaining outlaws.

As is often the case after a long period of anxiety and frustration, the final denouement was but a matter of seconds. Slade lowered his smoking Colts and peered through the powder fog at the three forms sprawled on the floor. He walked over and knelt beside the dying outlaw leader. Norton glared up at him with hellish hate, strove to speak, but choked on the blood welling in his throat, and choking, died!

Slade gazed down at him a moment, then straightened up.

"Guess this takes care of everything," he said in a tired voice. He slumped into one of the chairs and rolled a cigarette. Blount did likewise. Crane hauled out his pipe.

For some moments they smoked in silence, then took stock of the situation. The three owlhoots were satisfactorily dead. There was a very large sum of money on the table.

"The Marathon loot," Slade said. "The bank will be glad to receive it."

Blount was rummaging around the fireplace. "A lot of chuck here," he announced. "And coffee and a bucket of fresh water, and plenty of firewood. Suppose I make us a pot."

"That's a notion," Slade replied. "And while you're at it, Tom and I will get the rigs off those horses and flip the bits so our critters can graze and suck up some water at the spring over by the wall. The money we'll pack with us to town, but Lerner will send a cart in the morning to bring in the bodies."

"I'll guide 'em to 'em," Blount volunteered. "Before we leave, show me that crevice you've got the other carcass stuffed in."

The coffee was soon ready and was gratefully received. After which they headed for town to find Mary and Lerner anxiously awaiting them and profoundly thankful that nobody was hurt.

"And how do you feel, Walt?" Lerner asked.

"I feel as if I would like to do absolutely nothing for a week," Slade replied.

"Don't know just how your gal would go for that," said the sheriff, twinkling his eyes at her. Mary pointedly ignored him.

The following morning, Slade rode to the railhead to find much progress made.

"Because of which, you can look forward to a nice fat bonus in your pay envelopes," Slade told the workers. They cheered him till the walls of the nearly completed cut shook.

There was plenty of excitement when Norton's body was brought in and people learned he was the devilish outlaw leader who had terrorized the section for so long.

But it was nothing to what was to come. For two days later, the last scoopful of earth was cast aside and Echo had its railroad. Steel was hastily laid to accommodate the material train and Winona, Jaggers Dunn's private car that followed.

Slade at once repaired to the private car, where he shook hands warmly with Dunn and with old Sam, his colored chef and porter.

For quite a while they talked over various matters until Lerner summoned them to dinner.

"Have to be rolling to Chicago in the morning, but I'll be back," Dunn promised. He whispered to Mary, "Don't forget, I'm depending on you to put a stop to his gallivanting around so he can go to work for me and inherit this railroad empire."

"I'll do my best," the blue-eyed girl promised. And when, a couple of days later, with his kisses warm on her lips, she watched him ride away, tall and graceful atop his great black horse, she believed this time she was really making progress.